Lipstick Killah 2

Lock Down Publications and Ca$h Presents

Lipstick Killah 2

A Novel by *Mimi*

Lock Down Publications

P.O. Box 870494

Mesquite, Tx 75187

Visit our website @
www.lockdownpublications.com

First Edition July 2018
Printed in the United States of America

Lock Down Publications
Like our page on Facebook: Lock Down Publications @
www.facebook.com/lockdownpublications.ldp
Cover design and layout by: **Dynasty Cover Me**
Book interior design by: **Shawn Walker**
Edited by: **Sunny Giovanni**

Stay Connected with Us!

Text **LOCKDOWN** to 22828 to stay up-to-date with new releases, sneak peaks, contests and more…

.

Thank you.

For my best friend, Keesha, in honor of my God daughter, Zariyah.
R.I.P Zariyah
Sunrise 01-09-17 Sunset 01-25-17

Mimi

Chapter One

As Reign's eyes rolled to the back of her head, she just knew that it was over for her. *When did Senaj's brother get out of jail?* Reign thought. She had been gone for so long that she was out of touch with what was going on back in New York. Everything that was happening, she blamed herself, and at this point if Akuchi wanted to kill her then she was open to it. The moments that she had spent with Senaj spun around in her head and as she realized that she wouldn't be able to see his smile anymore, she confessed something to Akuchi. She was pregnant with Senaj's baby. She found out the last month in Florida and that's what pushed her to come back to New York.

"What did you just say?" Akuchi asked. The death grip that he had around Reign's neck was ripped from her body as a force knocked him off her.

The crash against the cabinets made Reign's eyes fly open and Jamori had Akuchi on his back with his hands now around Akuchi's neck.

Reign saw her grandmother and cousin Jackie standing at the doorway. She sat up and let it register that Jamori was about to kill her man's brother.

"Jamori stop!" She yelled trying to make her way over to them.

"Nah, Cuz! He was trying to kill you! Why would I do such a thing?" Jamori yelled.

"He's Senaj's brother! Get off him!"

"Reign, he was in here trying to murk ya' ass! No! Go take your ass somewhere."

Reign turned toward her grandmother and said, "Nana, you not gonna tell him nothing?"

"Sweetie, he's right. It doesn't matter who he is. If he's trying to hurt one of us, he got to go," her grandmother responded.

Reign knew that Senaj would never forgive her if she allowed her cousin to kill Akuchi. She sucked her teeth and went inside of her pantry and came back with a loaded nine. She walked up to Jamori and placed it to the back of his head. Jackie tried to move in on Reign, but Nana stopped her. Nana knew that Reign wouldn't pull the trigger and she needed Jackie to realize this.

"I told you to get off him. I hate having to pull my gun without using it, so cousin or not, if you want to live to talk about this, I suggest that you get your ass off him." Reign said with malice in her tone.

Jamori chuckled and said, "You better use that shit, Cuz; because whether you like it or not, it's lights out for this fool."

For a quick two seconds, Reign bounced the idea in her head. She knew she wouldn't be able to use it. Although she had just met her cousins, she had gotten close to them in the last four months and wouldn't want to have to harm either one of them. That was until she saw Akuchi's eyes rolling to the back of his head. She thought about Senaj and immediately raised her gun and brought it down on the back of Jamori's head, causing him to crumple on the side of Akuchi. Both Akuchi and Jamori laid there without moving and Reign made her way into the living room. She took a seat and placed her head back onto the couch.

Nana came in the living room shortly behind Reign after she had grabbed a few wet and dry paper towels from the kitchen. Jackie had gone to check on her brother.

"You okay?" Nana asked.

"Besides this headache, I guess I'm fine."

Jackie came inside of the living room with a scowl on her face and her arms folded across her chest. She looked at Reign and said, "My brother has a gash on the back of his head."

"He'll be fine. I only did enough damage to knock him out." Reign answered.

"But he's bleeding."

"Hush, girl, and just put something on the back of his head to stop the bleeding." Nana responded.

Jackie sucked her teeth and made her way into the kitchen, giving Nana some time to talk to Reign.

"Thank God we walked in when we did. You were almost gone, baby girl."

Reign exhaled and said, "I was almost going to accept death too. But I couldn't just let it end there. Nana, I found out that I am pregnant with Senaj's baby."

Nana chuckled. "I knew that too."

"How do you know everything?"

Jackie and Jamori walked in with Akuchi. His hands were zip-tied behind his back and Jackie said, "Because she nosy."

"Ya'll, his hands don't need to be zip-tied." Reign mentioned.

"Maybe yours should be." Jamori jumped in and said, holding a rag against his head.

"Jay, you pushed my hand and I really would have rather that you be knocked out than me putting a bullet in you."

The room got exceptionally quiet as everyone looked at each other wondering where to begin. Seeing that her cousins wasn't going to cut the zip-ties from Akuchi's hands, she got up and did so herself. Taking her seat next to Nana she spoke. "Akuchi, if I had known that it was you from the beginning, I think that we could have avoided this."

"Nah, it would have been the same. I knew who you were before I knocked on that door. I told my brother to watch you from the beginning. But no, he didn't want to listen to me. Now his ass is gone. Possibly dead right now as we are speaking." Akuchi spat with his voice dripping with hate.

"He's not dead," Reign said calmly.

"And how could you be so sure of that?" Akuchi roared.

Jamori stepped in and said, "You might want to pipe that down. My cousin isn't screaming and hollering at you so give her the same respect."

Akuchi's nostril's flared and although he was mad at the situation, he knew that he couldn't do nothing but respect what Jamori was telling him. "You right. And as much as I don't want to admit it, you do have a point. You could go ahead, Reign."

Reign looked between Jamori and Akuchi and she continued, "I know he's not dead. I feel it not only with my heart, but I feel it in my soul. I'm going to do everything in my power to find him, Akuchi. I never wanted this to happen and my uncle is going to pay for it."

"Wait a minute, you are telling me your uncle is behind this?"

"Yes. And I feel real fucked up. I don't know how he found out about Senaj. The only person besides these three people that knew I was dating Senaj was his two best friends and my best friend. We rarely went anywhere in public. I love Senaj with everything in me and I wouldn't want to put him in harm's way at all." Reign began to cry. This pregnancy thing was already getting on her nerves. She had never showed this much emotion in her life.

Nana stood up. "Listen, we are going to find Senaj. I have a clue as to where he might be."

"How, Nana?" Jackie asked.

Nana placed her hands behind her back. "It's a family warehouse that hasn't been used since KB was alive. I'm pretty sure that that's where James got him. Only because he knows that Reign doesn't know about it."

Jamori jumped up. "So what are we waiting on?"

At that moment, Reign's phone rang. Getting up from the couch, Reign walked to the entertainment center and grabbed her phone. She looked at the screen and rolled her eyes. She turned it to the group of people in the room and said, "It's James."

Mimi

Chapter Two

Senaj sat in the corner of a dark room exhausted. He hadn't slept since the night before he was kidnapped, and his mind had started to play tricks on him due to the lack of sleep. He had no clue where he was and all he wanted was to go home and get some sleep. Several times, Senaj replayed what happened at his graduation in his mind. He remembered seeing Reign's face in the crowd and even busting her gun, and he couldn't help but to think that she had something to do with it. Senaj got up from the corner he was in and walked to where the window was to see if he could see anything that would give an indication as to where he was. The windows were blacked out but not too dark as to where he couldn't see anything. All he saw was water. He punched the window in frustration and walked away from it.

The door of the room that he was in opened and a bright light shined in his face. He tried to see beyond the light, but the door closed behind him. He stood still where he was until there was a light that was turned on in the room. There was a guy there who was maybe five feet, eleven inches and was kind of on the built side with dark chocolate skin. The lines that rested on his forehead were a clear indication that he was stressed over something. Senaj backed against the wall, ready to stand his ground if need be. The room was eerily quiet as neither one spoke. Senaj waited for him to say something but it never came. Instead, he slid a phone out of his pocket and the light from it shone on his face. He tapped the screen a few times and the phone rang, indicating that he had called somebody.

"What's up?" It was Reign. Senaj's heart leaped in his chest at the sound of it. He felt mixed emotions because he had a feeling that she had something to do with it. On the other

13

hand, it had been four months since he had heard her voice and he didn't realize how much he missed it.

"Do you get it through your head now?" The guy asked.

"Get what through my head, James? You want something that I have no idea about. I honestly think that you made this up in your head," Reign said. When Reign said James, Senaj knew that this was the uncle that she told him about.

"You know and I know that that isn't even half the truth. I know that you have been gone for the past couple of months and I'm pretty sure that you have been searching for the same exact thing that I want."

"You're boring me with this conversation. Let Senaj go because he has nothing to do with anything. Be a man and face me. I'm the one that you're beefing with. Not him. If not, then like I said before, this fight will be to the death."

James chuckled and looked up at Senaj. "You see how she thinks she's tough? I should chop one of your fingers off just because she doesn't want to come to terms with me. I have been more than patient and now it's time to pay up, niece."

"Senaj, kick his ass if he tries to come near you! I promise I'm on my way to come get you!" Reign managed to yell before James hung up on her.

James looked up at Senaj and smirked. He began to walk out of the room but stopped as if he had an afterthought. "I can guarantee you that she won't find you here, unless she has some tracking device on you. I won't do anything to you now, but she has one more day to give me what I want, and if she doesn't, then I suggest you start praying to whatever God that you believe in."

"I have no doubt that she will come and find me. My girl is a beast and I hope and pray that she does you filthy when she sees you," Senaj said with an evil smirk. He wasn't quite confident about it, but he knew by the expression on James' face it affected him. James scrunched up his face, walked out of the room and slammed the door behind him. Senaj's mind ran with thoughts. He finally figured it out. Everything that Reign had told him was coming true and the only thing that came to his mind was the fact that he tried to do everything to get out of his "cell". *How could family members like this have beef this intense? What the fuck did I get myself into?* he thought. His conversation with his older brother Akuchi rang throughout his head. He should have listened to his brother from the beginning, then he wouldn't be in this situation. Walking towards the window again, he tried pushing the windows up and out to try and see if he could open them. With dismay, he gave up and backed up to the wall. He slid down, taking a seat. Senaj wasn't sure if Reign would come and get him and he decided that he should just come to grips with it that he wasn't going to get out of wherever it was James was holding him.

***

After speaking with her uncle on the phone, she couldn't help but to feel aggravated. She had gotten nowhere with the conversation. She went down to her basement and began to finish what she started as she grabbed her duffel bags of armory. She heard someone coming down the basement steps and turned her attention towards the stairs. Her grandmother descended with her arms folded across her chest. Without any words, Nana walked up to Reign and pulled her into a tight hug. The tears that stained Reign's face screamed that she was in desperate need of a hug. Reign tried with all her might to hold the cry in, but the hug felt so long overdue that Reign couldn't help but to take advantage and burst into tears. Snot and all.

"I know, baby. Get it out." Nana said rubbing her hand up and down Reign's back. She knew exactly what Reign was going through because she had been there more than once.

"Why me? Why Senaj? Nana, I swear I never meant to have him dragged into my mess. I'm afraid that once I get him, he won't have anything to do with me." She said in between hiccups.

Nana cleared her throat, grabbed Reign by her cheeks, and said, "If that man hasn't left you yet, he won't. He has already accepted you for who you are. Sure, he'll be mad but leaving you isn't going to happen. Right now, you need to get your emotions under control. You are now carrying a baby and you don't need to be stressing. I'm going to take these bags upstairs and we are going to head out. Let us handle this."

Reign's mouth dropped. She knew she couldn't let her family handle James. She wanted to be the one to end his life. She wanted him to look into her eyes and know that she was the reason why his life no longer would exist. She said, "No, Nana. I can't let ya'll do that. I need to do this for me."

"You're carrying a baby and I can't let you put my first great-grand at risk because you want to be a knuckle head."

"Nana, you don't understand."

Nana dropped the bags she held, dragged a chair over to them and pointed for Reign to sit down. The scowl that was on her face told Reign that she was serious. "I don't understand? Let me tell you something. I was hard-headed just like you when I had first learned the business. My father, your great-grandfather, God rest his soul, taught me everything that I knew. I was doing this way before you began at the age of sixteen. I don't mean training or getting ready to train; no. My first kill was at the age of sixteen. My father had his hand in a little bit of everything. One night, he took me out with him while my mother was sleeping. He said that he wanted me to get a firsthand look at the things that I would have to deal with."

"Not to cut you off, but are you sure that James isn't your son? He did this same thing to me, calling himself trying to tell me a story about my father." Reign said, slightly giggling.

Nana cut her eyes at Reign which halted her laughter instantly. Reign folded her hands into her lap and decided to shut her mouth until her grandmother was finished.

Nana continued, "Slimy snakes don't run in this family so don't you ever imply that dumb shit ever again in your life. Anyway. He took me to this warehouse; the same one that your uncle has your man in. I was tiny for my age, so my dad told me that if there was anything that was to go down, for me to stay up under this desk he had in his office. A few days prior, my mother saw that I was sick and had brought me to the doctor. What she thought was the flu, I was pregnant. She was beyond pissed with me. We hadn't told my father about it because my mother didn't know what it was that she wanted me to do. I was leaning more so to keeping it and she was leaning towards having me terminate it. She didn't want my father to know.

"As I watched my father down below, I realized that he was conducting a meeting with two men. One I knew right off the back was a little sketchy. Everything about him screamed bad vibes. But of course, I couldn't warn my dad. So, as I'm watching, I'm watching his movements and it's taking everything in me to not go downstairs. Long story short, I couldn't contain myself and I ran downstairs. By doing so, my father didn't realize what happened until it was done. The gun that my father always kept in the desk drawer was in my hand, and as the guy that I had been watching took his hand from out of his pocket with a .22 pistol. He raised his hand to shoot my father, but my father wasn't paying attention because he heard me coming. In a split second, I had raised my hand and shot him. I watched him drop as my gun wafted gun smoke in the air."

Reign sat at the edge of her seat, waiting for her Nana to finish the story.

Nana stood in front of Reign with her hands on her hips. "I should have listened to my father and stayed in that office. The other man that was with them drew his gun and shot me. Right in the stomach. My dad jumped on that guy so fast, snapping his neck with his bare hands. He came over to me to check on me. In that present moment, I welcomed death with open arms. I knew my baby was gone and I didn't want to live if I couldn't have my baby. I let my father know that I was pregnant, and the hurt that registered on his face broke me into tiny little pieces. He swooped me into his arms and told me that he was going to make sure that both the baby and I survived. Obviously, I was the only one who did. I only told you that story to tell you this. God forbid that you lose that baby; you will not forgive yourself for as long as you live. It eats away at you because you know you shouldn't have been in that position. You know you could have prevented losing that baby, yet and still you did what you wanted to do and didn't think about making sure that baby was safe."

Reign sat there silently as she watched her grandmother hurriedly swipe a tear from her eye. She understood where her grandmother was coming from but still, in her mind, she knew that she was going to do whatever it was she wanted to do. It was Reign's turn to give her Nana a hug.

The hug was interrupted by Jackie when she came down the stairs and said, "I don't know what's going on down here, but Reign, don't we have to go save your man?"

"Here we come Jackie." Reign shook her head.

Nana grabbed the duffel bags and they made their way back upstairs. Akuchi was standing by the window, looking out of it, shaking his head, and Jamori was sitting down watching the news. They were reporting the shooting at the graduation and the disappearance of Senaj. Reign walked over to the TV and turned it off, not being able to deal with it.

"If none of ya'll do the best that ya'll could to find my brother, or if he is dead by the time we get there, I promise I will gladly go to jail for multiple homicides," Akuchi said as he walked out of the house.

They all understood his pain but they all vowed silently that they would do everything to get Senaj back. Only on the strength of Reign. Seconds later, they followed Akuchi out. Nana took the driver's seat and everybody else climbed in. The ride was quiet with everyone in their own thoughts.

"How far is this warehouse?" Reign asked.

"It's in Jersey Shore. We should be getting there soon. We gonna have Jackie get a room in a hotel, and when night falls we'll head out," Nana responded.

"Sounds good to me," Jamori said.

"Good. We could get something to eat. It feels like I haven't eaten in years." Reign said, rubbing her stomach. She didn't have much but a little pouch.

Akuchi was stone cold quiet. He didn't know how they could all be so wrapped up in wanting to eat when there was a person, who happened to be his only other sibling, who needed to be found. He figured he would roll with the punches since he had no idea where this warehouse was and the fact that he didn't have any weapons to protect himself. He had yet to see or speak with his parents to make sure that they were okay. He knew that they were taking this hard. They were there firsthand to seeing their baby boy being kidnapped. The more he thought about it the more he was pissed about it.

Fifteen minutes later, Nana announced that they had arrived at the hotel. Jackie got out of the truck and went to go pay for a room. The guys grabbed the duffel bags and waited with Reign and her grandmother until she had to come out. Moments later, Jackie walked out letting them know that she had gotten the room and for them to follow her. They walked into the hotel and went up to the room without a problem. Once inside of the room, they began to devise a plan.

Chapter Three

After days of being away from her home, Pearl walked in and looked around. She halfway almost waited to hear Stanley's big mouth. That was until she realized that he was no longer around. She dropped her duffel bag and small suitcase at the door and walked into the kitchen to make herself something to eat. Opening the fridge, she grabbed some sandwich meat and cheese to only smell the meat and noticed that it went bad during the time that she was gone. She felt her baby doing flips and turns in her stomach, and she rubbed it to try and sooth the baby. Grabbing her cell phone, she decided to order Chinese food instead. After placing her order, she made her way into her room and instantly it was like what happened the night that she killed Stanley and the thing that he was cheating with, replayed in her mind.

"I think I will be switching rooms. I can't take this." She said out loud to herself.

Pearl was forced to leave the hotel that she was in since Reign had up and disappeared and stopped the payments on her room. She tried calling Reign but was met with a dead end when the phone service said that the number was changed. For four months she hadn't seen her best friend and she missed her. Every day since Senaj came and confronted her, she regretted ever telling that bold face lie to Reign. She knew she was wrong and she wanted to come clean to Reign and tell her the truth, but she couldn't because she had no idea where she was.

Pearl grabbed a bunch of her clothes and made it to her guest bedroom and decided that while she was waiting for her food, she would take a shower and get comfortable.

While in the shower, Pearl thought about all the things that had happened to her in the last few months. She had been so close to living out her dream of becoming a rap star but that was taken right from under her. Until that very day, she still had no idea why they decided not to sign her. Figuring that she would never be able to have a chance like that again, she planned on searching for a job that following day. She had no father for her child and she had to do what she saw her mother do when raising herself and two of her other siblings. She had to admit that her mother did the best that she could do as a single parent, and Pearl decided that she would do just the same.

Climbing out of the shower, she placed a robe around her body and got ready to get dressed. There was a knock on the door, so getting dressed had to wait. She carefully rushed to the door with her money in hand as she got ready to pay for her food. The delivery guy gave her the food and went about his business. She took the food into the living room and sat down. Turning the TV on, there was a piece of paper with a note written on it laying on top of the carton. Picking it up, she read the note and instantly wanted to throw up.

The note said that they knew what she did to Stanley and that whoever it was that read the note would make sure that she would get what she had coming to her. Her hands shook as she had second thoughts about eating the food that she had just ordered. Whoever this was that was sending her this note could have easily slipped something into her food. Tears stained her cheeks as she instantly forgot about the note and got upset about not being able to eat her food. She walked into the kitchen and threw it in the trash and took something from the freezer to cook. The note rested on the coffee table as she walked back into the room to get dressed.

"One way or another, I am going to find out who the hell sent this note," Pearl said grabbing her cell phone. Hitting a series of buttons, she took a seat on the bed and waited for the person to pick up the phone.

"Who's this?" He asked.

"I need to speak with you," she said into the phone.

"Yet again I ask, who is this?"

Exhaling, she said, "This is Pearl."

"What do you have to speak to me about? Last time I checked, you ain't fuck with me like that." He mentioned.

"Look. I just need to speak with you face to face. I have some questions that I need answered and I think you would be the only one who could help."

"I'm kind of busy. Could this wait?"

"Absolutely not. Be at my house in an hour." Pearl hung up.

Taking her robe off, she grabbed her coconut oil and rubbed it all over her body. Her biggest fear was getting stretch marks in places that she didn't want them, and she tried her hardest to avoid them. She got dressed in booty shorts and a t-shirt that barely covered her seven-month-old belly. Making her way once back into the living room, she took a seat and went through the channels. The news station caught her attention. They were reporting the shooting at the med school graduation. She sat up on the edge of her couch and listened as they played a clip of what happened. Her mouth dropped open as she saw Senaj being dragged off the stage. Before the video ended, the person recording panned across the scene and for a split second she saw a woman who closely resembled Reign.

"What the fuck is going on?" She asked out loud to herself. Thoughts ran rampant in her head, and before she knew it she tried to piece everything together, and there was her guest banging on her door.

Struggling to get off the couch, she waddled to the door and opened it. He walked in and went straight into the living room without so much as a hello.

Closing the door, she yelled behind him, "Well hello to you!"

"What you called me down here for? I have things that I have to tend to."

"James, cut it out. You and I both know you don't have nothing important to do."

"Girl, come on with it." He said with irritation in his voice.

Taking a seat on the couch next to James she began to speak. "A few months back, I killed my boyfriend."

James smiled. "What? No shit? Since when you became about that life?"

"Since I got tired of him humiliating me and cheating right in my bed with a tranny."

James looked her up and down and stopped at her belly. His eyebrows raised. "That's his baby you are carrying?"

"No, it's yours," she responded with a straight face.

James' eyes almost popped out of their sockets as he began to stammer, trying to get his words together. "What? How is that my baby? We haven't slept together in months."

Watching James sweat, Pearl enjoyed him panicking. Moments later she almost slid off the couch due to her laughing so hard. In between her laughs she said, "Nigga, please. This ain't your baby."

"Why would you even play around like that, Pearl? That shit ain't funny," he whispered through gritted teeth, holding his right hand over his heart.

"I would have been told you if this was your baby. Now, shut up and listen."

James stood up. "Aiight. Go ahead and speak."

"Like I was saying, I killed him and the woman-man that he was cheating with. I called Reign over to help me clean up. That was the night that we went over to your house. I had to tell her how you tried to have me set her up and so forth, only because I had to reveal that I knew what she did for a living. I needed her help and I want to apologize to you for that."

"So that was you that started this mess with me and my niece?" he asked with fire dancing in his eyes.

"No! Hell no! She was pissed with you way before I even told her about you trying to set her up. For what reason, I can't even begin to tell you why. The only reason I'm telling you this is because I need your help. Somebody knows what I did, and they are putting notes in my food. Food that I am having delivered."

"Well, what you want me to do about it?"

Pearl thought about her answer. She didn't know what she wanted James to do about it. She asked instead, "Have you heard from Reign? I know that ya'll got this beef going on but maybe she would have reached out to you because of this stuff that's going on with her man?"

James' ears perked. "What you mean the stuff that's going on with her man?"

"I just saw on the news that he was kidnapped the day of his graduation, right off stage as he was accepting his diploma. What fucked me up the most was that I slightly caught a glimpse of someone who looked like Reign, but I wasn't sure. She's been missing for months now and to be quite honest, I'm kind of worried." Pearl stated.

"Reign is back." James simply said. He walked to the window and looked out of it. He knew the story made the news but if the news stations had a video clip of what happened, there was a possibility that there was a video with his face on it.

"What do you mean Reign is back? How do you know that?" Pearl inquired, walking up next to James by the window.

James folded his hands across his chest. "I kidnapped her man. I wasn't expecting for her to be there because she was MIA. I figured that if I kidnapped him, she would come out of hiding. She almost got my ass, but the bullet whizzed right passed my head. I mean it was so close I heard the wind with it. I need a big favor from you. If you help me out, I promise that I will help you with this issue with who is sending you notes with your food."

Pearl raised her eyebrow as she watched James inch closer to her. "What kind of favor?"

"I need you to get in contact with Reign. I need another day so that I could wrap some things up and I need for her to stay far away from trying to find her nigga. Give me your phone so that I could give you her number."

Pearl did what James asked her. Handing it back to her she asked, "Well, what do I tell her to make sure to keep her busy?"

"Tell her about this issue with somebody sending you notes. Exaggerate a little bit. If she's supposed to be your friend, then it should be easy for her to come to your rescue."

Pearl's mind got the best of her and the wheels began to turn. She walked away from James and wrapped her arms around herself as if she was trying to keep herself warm. She stood in front of the TV and said, "I don't think this is going to work."

James walked up behind her. He was so close that she felt his manhood on her ass and instantly her panties got moist. The smell of his Gucci Guilty Intense cologne seeped into her nostrils and did something to her. She hadn't had any attention from a man in months, and at that moment she craved James.

Her mind took her to that place, even if she didn't want to. James whispered in her ear, "Why not?"

With her eyes closed, she responded, "Before she left, I tried to get her man to have sex with me. I was hormonal. I haven't been touched by a man in what seemed like forever. I told her that it was all his fault. He came onto me. Senaj confronted me so I know that she knows that it was all me. I doubt that she is going to come to my rescue."

"If all you needed was some dick, you could have called me." He wrapped his arms around the front of her body and gripped both her breasts in each hand. He placed his lips on the nape of her neck and kissed her. Her body shook internally, and she just knew she felt her juices leaking down her leg.

"I wish it was that easy, James. You shot out my window so I'm pretty sure that you wouldn't have come to give me some dick."

"How would you know that if you didn't try? I'm here now and look who's ready to serve you some dick." James turned Pearl around so that she could face him.

He looked her in her eyes as his hand wrapped around her neck and he slightly squeezed the sides, causing her mouth to open. He placed his lips against hers and kissed her with passion. Her knees got weak as she was ready to let them buckle right from under her. Pulling away from her, James took her by the hand and began to lead her to her bedroom. Reluctantly, she followed behind him.

Inside of her bedroom, James instructed for her to lay on the bed. With her swollen belly, she laid down. James walked between her legs, took her boy shorts off and flung them across the room. He bent her legs so that her knees were in the air. Pearl's breathing got heavier as James kneeled in front of her opened legs. Spreading them just enough so that he could fit his shoulders and head between her legs, he used his index finger to slide it up and down in between her lips, just enough to rub her clit as well. James placed kisses on her inner thighs as he inserted two fingers deep inside her folds. Pearl moaned and raised her shirt to extract her breasts from her bra.

James' tongue pushed through her second set of lips as he flicked it across her clit softly. He worked his fingers in and out of her and her juices leaked all over them. Wrapping his lips around her clit, he softly nibbled on it, causing her moans to get louder. His tongue and fingers worked faster as Pearl's body shook as she was coming close to her climax. Pearl began to move her hips into his face as her mouth dropped and she was cumming all over his face.

James got up from between her legs and took his clothes off. They made eye contact and James winked at her as he took his shorts off. Kicking his boxers off, he reached into his pants pockets and pulled out a condom. Before he placed it on his rod, he stroked himself. The blood pumped through the veins on the shaft of his penis as he studied Pearl who had reached in between her legs to swirl her fingers in her honey pot.

Walking closer to the bed, James closed Pearl's legs and placed her on her side. He slid the condom on and climbed on the bed behind her. Pearl's breath was caught in her throat as she looked at James over her shoulder. Kissing her on the shoulder, he elevated her left leg over his waist and held his dick steady. Her pinkness swallowed him whole once he was able to move past her tightness. As he moved his hips, guiding himself in and out of Pearl, his arm wrapped around her waist and grabbed her breast in his hand.

"Damn! Out of all these years that I've been getting pussy I have never experienced pregnant pussy," James said. He finally was able to see what all the fuss was about with pregnant pussy. Pearl was super wet and was leaking juices on them both.

"Shit!" Pearl moaned as she felt herself ready to cum yet again.

"You think if I turned you over with your ass up, you could do it?" James asked as he pumped in and out of Pearl.

"We could try and see." Pearl, at this point, didn't care if she could or not. She wasn't going to let her round belly get in the way of receiving the best dick that she has had in months.

Pearl got on her hands and knees as she arched her back just until her belly touched the bed. James watched from the bottom of the bed as her sex opened, calling his name. Wiping sweat from his forehead, he tugged at her ankles to let her know to come further down to the bottom of the bed. She did so as James grabbed both of her ass cheeks and gripped them. He watched as his dick entered her, causing him to close his eyes as she tightened around his length. He moved into her slowly, biting down on his bottom lip.

James moaned under his breath as he felt himself becoming light headed because the pussy was so good. His body tensed up as he felt himself getting ready to bust his nut. Pearl was throwing her ass back as if she wasn't pregnant.

"Pearl?" James whispered.

"Mmm, yes?" Pearl answered with her eyes closed.

"I'm about to nut. Turn around and open your mouth."

She moved as quickly as she could. She sat back on her knees and opened her mouth wide as James snatched the condom off and jerked his meat off until his thick white cream landed in her mouth and on her face. His body shook as he watched her catch his nut, turning him on even further.

Pearl used her index finger to gather his nut that was on her face and inserted her finger in her mouth. She winked at him as she said, "Ahhh. Protein."

"You a nut and a half. Swear I missed that pussy and it's even better now that you got a baby in you." James smirked. He sat on the bed and began to get dressed.

"Leaving so soon?"

"Yes. I told you before I got here and when I got here that I had things to do. Can you do what I asked you? If you do, you will continue to get this dick."

"I can try, James. I don't know how she would feel about speaking with me."

"All that I ask is that you try."

"Okay. I could do that." She watched as James finished getting dressed.

He walked over to her and placed a kiss on her forehead. He began to walk out of the door but paused as if he forgot something. Pearl watched as he went inside his pocket and peeled a few hundred dollar bills off and placed it on the bed in front of her. With a wink, James left without another word. Pearl sat on the bed debating on whether she should contact Reign or not. She did tell James that she would try, so that's what she did. She grabbed her cell phone and looked through her contacts and landed on Reign. Pushing the call button, she held her breath as the phone rang in her ear.

Chapter Four

The hotel room was quiet as everybody sat around either on their phones, reading, or looking at TV. The butterflies in Reign's stomach wouldn't stop because she was so nervous. She couldn't help but to pace across the floor. Night fall was coming soon and the only thing she wanted to do was get her man, share the good news about him being a daddy, and continue with her life.

Jackie excused herself to go to the bathroom as she had been holding her pee since before they left Reign's house. As she was wiping and getting off the toilet, there was a knock on the door. "Somebody is in here," she called out, flushing the toilet.

The door opened and Akuchi stuck his head through the door. He said, "I know. I was wondering if you had a moment."

Jackie looked around the bathroom. "In here? Why not out there?"

"Your cousin is out there wearing the carpet thin and working my nerves."

Jackie rolled her eyes. She sighed. "I guess it wouldn't hurt. Come in."

Akuchi walked in and closed the door behind him. Jackie closed the lid of the toilet and sat while Akuchi stood against the sink. Akuchi began, "I just wanted to know if you knew exactly what the plan was. I saw you speaking with your grandmother and your brother."

Jackie cleared her throat and spoke. "No. We don't have no real plan except to bombard the warehouse and to make sure that Reign doesn't get in the way. She's a bit hard headed and all we want is for her to stay out of the way until we get Senaj."

"I can't believe that this is what I had to come home to." Akuchi seethed. He had every right to be mad.

"If you were just getting home, how did you know what happened to Senaj so fast?"

"I was going to surprise him by showing up to his graduation. I got there, and I saw everything go down. I realize now that I had no right to attack your cousin the way that I did. I saw her busting her guns at whoever; well Reign's uncle. I was just heated. I told him to be careful while fucking with Reign, but he didn't listen."

"Listen. I'm just meeting my cousin for the first time, four months ago. She is in love with your brother and I am quite sure that she wouldn't allow anything to happen to your brother on purpose. Oh, and her uncle just so happens to be mine and Jamori's father."

With a chuckle, Akuchi said, "I guess every family does have its secrets. I just want to get my brother and make sure that he's good. He is the only sibling that I have, and I was already gone for damn near fifteen years because of a dumb choice. It's been so long since I've seen him, and I don't know how I would live if something was to happen to him."

Jackie looked up at Akuchi and saw that his eyes had become a little misty. She stood up and grabbed his hand into hers. She liked her lips and looked at him in his eyes. She whispered, "You have to trust us, which is something that I know you are going to have a hard time doing because you're just meeting us. But you have to know that we are more than capable of getting your brother."

Before Akuchi could respond, there was a knock on the door. Nana peeked her head through the door and looked at Akuchi and Jackie through squinted eyes. She asked, "And just what the hell is going on in here?"

"Nothing, Nana. I was just reassuring Akuchi that we would get Senaj."

"That's all that better be going on in here."

Akuchi watched as Jackie rolled her eyes. He interrupted. "I'm pretty sure that you could understand my concerns. I just got a little worried because I saw that you guys were huddled around, and nothing was happening."

"Yes, I do understand. Akuchi, we must go through with this delicately only because I had absolutely no time to case out the warehouse. We don't know how many people he got surrounded or even so on the inside. Just try to trust us. Anyway, I came to tell ya'll to come on, we about to leave. Put the gloves on, Jamori is about to wipe everything down that we could have touched."

Jackie and Akuchi walked from out of the bathroom while eyeing each other. Jackie's stomach and fluttered with butterflies as they placed the gloves on their hands. Jamori was spraying some blue liquid around the room while franticly wiping everything down.

Reign stood in her own zone as she strapped a bullet proof vest on. She had her two-rose gold Maxim 9's in a holster and placed on a black leather jacket.

"Everybody ready?" Nana asked. Met with silence she knew that they were ready.

Walking to the door, they left in a single file as they headed toward the nearest staircase to exit. Death was about to rock Jersey Shore.

Outside of the staircase, Reign's phone vibrated against her butt, being that it was held in her pants pocket. Her eyebrows furrowed, and she looked at the screen. She didn't recognize the number, but she decided on answering it anyway. It could have been Senaj calling to let her know that he had escaped from James.

"Hello?" Reign answered.

Reign was met with silence until on the other end, there was rustling and then breathing. The person said, "Reign?"

"Who the fuck is this?" Reign asked into the phone. She knew the voice but couldn't place it.

Hearing the hostility in Reign's voice, everybody stopped in their tracks to see what was going on.

"It's Pearl. Listen, I know you haven't heard from me in a long time and I just wanted to tell you that I was sorry about the thing that happened with Senaj. I really miss my best friend and I need you right now. I'm only getting further in my pregnancy, and with each day I realize that I don't have anyone. Please. I just need you to come over for a little while." Pearl spoke, sniffling.

"Pearl? How did you get my number?"

"Is that really the first thing that you say to me after months of not talking to me?" Pearl asked with a slight attitude.

"Listen, girl, right now is not the time to catch an attitude. I got shit to do. I'll holla at you another time," Reign said and hung the phone up. For a few seconds longer, she looked at the phone until the screen went black. She placed her phone back where it was and waved her hand for everyone to continue. She felt it vibrate, ignoring it. Dealing with Pearl was going to have to be put on the back burner for the time being.

Reaching the ground level, they left out as smoothly as they had entered and climbed into the truck.

Fifteen minutes later, they were parking four blocks from the warehouse. They climbed out in silence and checked their guns, making sure they were locked with one in the chamber. Nana looked over at everyone and paused when she got to Reign. She hated to do this but she knew it was going to have to get done if she wanted her first grandchild to make it into this world.

"Reign, we need you to stay back. I've let you come this far because I know that you could be stubborn just like your daddy. I don't need anything happening to the baby." Nana spoke with concern.

Rolling her eyes and placing her hands on her hips, Reign reluctantly decided to listen to her grandmother this one time. She knew that Senaj would be looking for her, but then again Akuchi was there, so she figured that it would be good enough. She finally said, "Okay, Nana. Just know that I'm giving ya'll ten, maybe fifteen minutes tops to get inside that warehouse. I'm gonna drive up and watch the front. My man gets hurt, I'm gonna forget that ya'll family and light ya'll asses up like the fourth of July."

While Nana didn't like the threat, she nodded in agreement. She knew her granddaughter was in love and she couldn't blame her. She hugged Reign and motioned for everyone to follow her.

Reign climbed inside the truck and beat the steering wheel with closed fists. That had been one of the hardest things that she ever had to do. Sitting back in her seat, she took her cell phone out to watch the clock. There were several missed calls and text messages from Pearl. She didn't open the messages, but she saved the number. Her mind wandered as to how Pearl had gotten her new phone number. She then realized that James was the only one in New York who had her number, and somehow, Pearl had gotten it from him. Reign's nostrils flared as she thought about Pearl betraying her yet again. She knew she would have to see Pearl soon, and if she had to, it wouldn't be a pretty visit.

Noticing that fifteen minutes passed, she started the truck and turned the headlights off. She slowly made her way to the warehouse and parked. Reaching into the back seat, she picked up the M4 with the scope and suppressor. She watched her surroundings like a hawk, making sure nobody tried to run into the warehouse. All was quiet until Reign jumped at the first round of bullets. She looked around and didn't see anyone.

Reign sat up straight as she waited. It felt like hours had passed before all the gun fire seized. Reign watched the doors of the warehouse, watching intently. A figure emerged and began walking towards the car. Fixing the gun against her shoulder, Reign looked through the scope and noticed that it was Akuchi. She jumped out of the truck and began to run toward him. She feared that she lost her newfound family.

"Akuchi! What happened? Where is my cousins and my grandmother?" She asked ready to bust out into a full-blown crying baby.

"Relax. They're fine. They got James and Senaj. They sent me out here to come get you because they wanted Senaj to see the both of us. Your grandmother was hit but she took that shit like a true G."

"What do you mean my grandmother was hit? Where was she hit?"

Akuchi chuckled and said, "It was only a graze. Relax. I must get the first aid kit from the back of the truck. After that we can go in. You need to relax."

Reign walked with Akuchi back to the truck. Playing with her fingernails, she asked, "Do you know how he is? Is he okay? Did James put his hands on him?"

"I don't know, Reign. I didn't get a chance to see him. Stop rambling and let's get inside. I get that you're anxious 'cause I am too, but you know what? It's got to get done."

"Yeah, you right. Let's go." Reign swung the gun across her shoulder by the strap that was attached to it.

They began their walk into the warehouse as their hearts beat from their chests. Reign froze up when she heard Senaj's voice in the distance asking who her family members were. Reign and Akuchi walked toward their voices and entered the room. Reign entered first, staring Senaj down.

"Reign?" Senaj asked. He began to walk toward her.

Reign took the gun from around her and ran full speed at Senaj. She jumped into his arms while laughing and crying at the same time. "I'm so sorry for getting you into this mess. I've missed you so much you have no idea." Reign whispered as she placed kisses on his cheek and his neck.

"I've missed you too, baby girl. If we both good that's all that matters. I just can't wait until we get home. I'm hungry, thirsty, tired; shit, all of the above." He said causing her to laugh.

Akuchi walked into the room, clearing his throat. He said, "I hope I could get a hug like that. I've been gone longer than ya'll even been together. Way longer."

"Chi!" Senaj smiled, bringing happiness into his heart. He missed Reign no doubt, but his brother was another story. He walked up to his older brother and hugged him as tight as he could.

It brought tears to everybody eyes. Neither Senaj or Akuchi could hold back their tears.

"When did you get home?" Senaj asked.

Akuchi cleared his throat. "Bro, we could talk about that when we get to the crib. Your girl over there been itching to get to her uncle. I think we should at least let her get to him."

Senaj raised his eyebrow and watched as Akuchi walked toward the crew that saved him. He handed the first aid kit that he was holding over to Jamori, and he began to tend to his grandmother's wound.

Senaj walked over to Reign and hugged her from behind. She began to speak. "Jackie, where is James?"

"He's upstairs in the same room that Senaj was in. I don't think that you should do this, Reign." Jackie spoke as she was concerned about her baby cousin just as was her Nana.

"Listen. Ya'll stopped me from helping get Senaj. Ya'll not stopping me from doing this."

Senaj looked on as Reign began to walk away. Jamori stayed with Nana as everyone else followed behind Reign. She walked up to the door and kicked it down. Literally. She walked in and went straight for James and delivered a fierce upper cut that sent James and the chair that he was sitting on flying. When he landed, Reign stood over him and wrapped her hand around his neck. She lifted him up and off his feet as everybody watched on, amazed at her strength. James' feet swung, and his hands scratched at her hands as she stared at him teary eyes.

"You of all people! I trusted you! You gave me thanks by setting me up and trying to get some money that I had no idea about! I looked at you as a father figure once my dad died and this is the thanks I get?" Reign yelled. Without much effort she threw James against the wall and James collapsed, banging his head along the way to the ground. She ran over and delivered a swift kick to his ribs.

"Reign. I get that you you're upset. I deeply apologize, but that can't change nothing. I just want to walk out of here with my life. I promise if you let me go, I will leave the state. You won't have to worry about me fucking with you no more."

"You got one thing right! I won't have to worry about you, 'cause nigga you are dying tonight!" Reign said. She curled her hand into a fist and got ready to punch him square in the face, when he moved, and her hand crashed right into the wall. Her middle finger knuckle and ring finger knuckle were broken in the process.

Akuchi walked further into the room but his arm was grabbed by Jackie. She silently shook her head as she assured him that Reign would be just fine.

James hobbled and tried to make his way to stand up straight. Reign ignored the pain shooting through her hand as she raised her foot and slammed it into his chest. He fell again, and this time Reign allowed him to lay there to get his bearings together. Nana and Jamori managed to join them as everybody entered fully into the room and watched Reign do what she had to do.

Nana sucked her teeth and shook her head. She asked, "Why would ya'll let this girl do this?"

"She has every right, does she not?" Senaj asked, folding his arms across his chest. He wanted more than anything to stop Reign from doing what she was doing. In his eyes James had this shit coming and he knew that with or without Senaj's input, Reign's mind was set, so who was he to stop her.

Nana looked at Senaj and simply shook her head.

James got up and faced reality. He wasn't leaving out of that warehouse alive. He looked at his twins and regretted sending them to go live with their grandmother. They should have been taking his side, but instead they were on their cousin's side. The scowls that they wore on their faces let him know just how much they had for him.

Blood dripped from the corners of his mouth as he began to laugh hysterically. "I should have convinced your mother to get the abortion a little harder. I didn't want you little niggas!" He yelled with laughter.

Jackie tried to charge past Jamori, Akuchi, and Senaj.

Reign ran up to James and kneed him in his stomach. "Get your pussy ass up! I'm tired of fighting alone!" Reign yelled.

James stood up yet again as he put his hands in front of his face to block it. Leaning into his punch, he jabbed her in her mouth, causing her lip to split and blood seeped through the crack. Reign smiled as she bounced on the tips of her toes like a skilled boxer. She extended her arm, faking a right and sent a left crashing down on his jaw. His bones shattered upon impact, causing James to spit several teeth across the floor. Reign followed that up with a kick to the nuts and as he came down, Reign kneed him in the face, breaking his nose. James fell onto his back as he panted, trying to catch his breath.

Jackie, while no one was paying attention, ran into the room and kicked him in the face, rattling his brain. She yelled, "That was for me and my brother! You were never shit and I couldn't be gladder that you sent us to my grandmother! I wish this was my battle because, nigga, you would have been dead."

"Jackie, get back and let Reign finish. We need to be getting out of here soon," Nana said sternly.

Jackie backed up with tears in her eyes. Reign reached for her Maxim 9's and aimed them at James. Before she pulled the trigger, all the good memories she shared with James invaded her thoughts. The tears started once again, and James took this moment to swoop his foot up under Reign, causing her to fall and land harshly on her back. He jumped at this moment and climbed on top of Reign and began to choke her. Only for a quick second, a bullet straight to his dome caused his head to explode all over Reign.

Reign pushed James off her, wiping his thoughts from her face. She looked up towards the group and noticed that Senaj held the gun that saved her. Reaching into her pants pocket, she took out her signature Louboutin lipstick and drew a heart on his wrist and stood up. Reign walked up to Senaj and grabbed her gun from him. With a hug, they all filed out of the room, leaving the James laying in the middle of the floor.

Mimi

Chapter Five

Akachi and Zane sat at their youngest sons' kitchen table with worry. They hadn't slept since Senaj was taken from his ceremony, and the police hadn't been any help. They didn't have an idea as to even began to think where to look for Senaj. They feared the worst. That was until they heard the doorbell ringing. Both of Senaj's parents got up and practically ran to the door, hoping that it was the police coming with some good news. It was an even bigger shock when they opened the door and it was Senaj with Reign. Zane screamed with tears of joy as she wrapped Senaj in a hug. Reign moved out of the way. She knew that once his parents found out what happened and her involvement, that they were going to hate her.

"Oh, I am so glad you are okay, son," Zane said as she dragged him inside of the living room.

At that moment, Akuchi walked in and told Reign that her grandmother wanted her. As Reign walked away, Akuchi walked into the living room and watched as his parents hugged on Senaj. A smile spread across his face when he decided to clear his throat. His parents turned their attention toward him and his mother was the first to make it over to him. They hugged him so tight, and his mother couldn't stop her tears from falling.

"Good to have you home, Akuchi," his father said, not being able to hold his tears back.

"Um, hello. I am still sitting here." Senaj complained like a child.

Laughing, they walked into the living room and sat down with Senaj, asking him questions about what happened. He recounted the story about what happened, and his parents couldn't help to feel angry with Reign. Although she didn't have anything to do with the kidnapping, her involvement and the reason their son was taken was because of her dealings. She had put their baby boy in great danger and they wanted the relationship to end immediately.

"Mom, dad, I get what you guys are saying but I'm an adult and I need to figure this thing out by myself. I know you guys are worried, but I'm sure that I will be okay. For now, I just want to eat, take a shower, and get some rest," Senaj spoke.

His parents nodded in understanding as Senaj got up and excused himself.

Reign walked in and followed him to his room. She knew that sooner rather than later she was going to have to face his parents. At that moment, it wasn't the best time.

Upon entering the room, Senaj stripped out of his clothes and Reign leaned her back against the door. So many things ran through her head as she searched for the right words to begin with. The look on Senaj's face clearly said that he was pissed off.

"Babe, I- I don't even know where to begin. I swear if I would have any thought in my mind that James would have stooped this low, I would have been handled him." Reign began as she walked to the bed where Senaj sat, taking her shoes off. His head was in his hands and the moment she rubbed her hand across his back, it sent chills down his spine.

"But you had an idea that it could possibly happen? You know what kind of business you deal with. Hell, I don't even know what you do, but I know enough to know that when some shit goes down, either somebody dies, gets hurt, or gets taken. You can't tell me you had no idea that it could get to this." Senaj spoke with irritation in his tone.

"Of course, I knew that this could have happened, but if I would have known that he would have went this far, then—"

"Then what, Reign! There was nothing that you could have done to stop it. Especially not when you decided to up and leave." Senaj mentioned as he got up from the bed.

"Senaj, I had my reasons to leave."

"Before you actually heard my side of the story? You just took that bitch's word as gospel and didn't think once to hear me out. What type of shit is that? That is not how adults in relationships work shit out. I sat there and listened to you when you told me about what you did for a living. You didn't even blink to even give me a chance to tell you my side of what happened!" Senaj yelled.

The tears rained down Reign's face. She knew that Senaj was right and she couldn't even begin to dispute it. Reign knew that she would have given him that much and she felt horrible that she didn't. "Yes, I admit I was wrong for not allowing you to tell me your side. I have a hard time dealing with shit like this, and my first instinct is to always run to not deal with the bullshit. I'm sorry, Senaj. I don't know what else to say. I just want to move on from this mess."

Senaj looked over his shoulder at Reign and said, "I wish the same thing, Reign. But you weren't the one who was put into this situation. Not knowing if you are going to live or die isn't like trying to figure out if you want a burger or a chicken sandwich."

Reign walked up to Senaj, ready to hug him from behind, but he moved, causing Reign's mouth to drop open. She said, "Please, don't do this."

"Go home. I need some time to myself." Senaj walked out of the room, heading to the bathroom for a shower.

Reign's heart dropped to the bottom of her stomach. Her heart felt like it was being torn in a million pieces. Turning to place her shoes on her feet, she rushed out of the apartment unnoticed and walked aimlessly. She hadn't even told Senaj that he was going to be a father. She didn't even know if now would had been the right time. Going home and giving Senaj some space would be her best option.

***

The next morning, Senaj woke up with a pounding headache. The sun shined brightly on his face through the window, causing Senaj to throw the covers back over his face. Zane, at the dinner table the night before, told Senaj that he needed to contact the police to let them know what happened. In the back of Senaj's mind, that would not happen. He knew if he did say something to the police, it would not only put Reign at risk, but himself as well. He was the one that pulled the trigger, killing James. No way in hell would he go to the police.

There was a knock on the door that caused Senaj to remove the covers from his face. In walked his brother. Rolling his eyes, he placed his head back under the covers, wishing that he could go back to sleep.

"How are you feeling, baby brother?" Akuchi asked, taking a seat on the bed.

"Like shit."

"As to be expected after the shit that you just went through. How did it go with Reign?"

Senaj sighed. He didn't want to speak about Reign. He knew, in his mind, that they were done. His heart, not so much. Senaj said, "We got into it last night. I don't think that we could be together. I told her from the jump, when she first told me what she did for a living, that I didn't want to get caught up in this mess. I told her my career was important and she agreed that shit wouldn't get out of hand. I don't think I could trust her."

Akuchi snatched the covers off Senaj and made him sit up. Although Akuchi didn't like the situation to begin with, he had liked how down Reign was for his brother. He saw in

Reign what he never saw in Senaj's past girlfriends. "Listen, I can't tell you what to do with your relationship, but I damn sure could give you some advice. I was skeptical about Reign and I had my doubts, but she showed me that she is down for you. That girl loves the shit out of you, and it's rare that you get someone like that. You know how many stories I've heard about in prison, where these niggas' girls say they gonna hold him down while he does his time, but go behind their backs and fuck they homie? Reign ain't like that and I think that you should talk to her at least one last time before you actually give up all the way."

Senaj had to admit that his brother was right. Senaj watched as Akuchi walked out of the room. Agreeing with his heart, Senaj decided that after he went to go see his school officials he would go to see Reign. Climbing out of the bed, Senaj got his clothes ready for the day as he went to go shower. In the shower, he thought about the past two days and had to thank God that he was able to come out of that situation without injury. One thing that sat on his conscience was the fact that he had killed. He had killed in the name of love. It was fight or flight for him, and while he knew that his girl would be able to handle herself, at that moment he also thought that he would lose her. The sound of the gun going off in his head snapped him out of his thoughts and made him realize that the water was beginning to get cold. He washed and got out to only get dressed and join his family.

Meanwhile

"Reign, let's go! Get up. We need to get you to the doctor to make sure that everything is okay with the baby." Jackie spoke, trying to grab the covers from Reign.

"No! I don't want to go!" Reign yelled like a child.

"I'm telling Nana!" Jackie folded her arms across her chest.

Reign sat up in bed and moved the covers from her face. She laughed. "You do realize that I'm a grown ass woman and she can't make me do something that I don't want to do."

Jackie smirked. "Nanaaaaaa! Reign in here talking 'bout she a grown ass woman and that you can't tell her what to do! She doesn't want to go to the doctor! Oh, and Nana she said your gumbo taste like dirty socks!"

"Ooh, you stupid bitch!" Reign yelled, climbing out of the bed.

Nana came in the room with her arms folded. "How old are ya'll?"

"Grown." Reign responded.

"Twenty-Eight." Jackie lowered her head.

"So, act like it. Reign, I don't care if I have to make you go by dragging you by that long ass Brazilian woman's hair you have on your head, you're going." Nana glared at them before she left the room.

Reign rolled her eyes and reluctantly dragged herself from the bed. "Snitchin ass bitch," she mumbled, causing Jackie to giggle.

Reign headed toward the bathroom, turning the water on as hot as it could go. She stood in front of her floor-length mirror and admired herself as she took her clothes off. Just a few days ago, she didn't have a belly, but now as she looked upon herself, she saw her baby pudge. A smile crept upon her face and she rubbed her belly. Making the silent decision to tell Senaj about their baby after her appointment, Jackie walked in, holding Reign's ringing phone.

"You could have knocked!" Reign exclaimed, covering her breasts and vagina with her hands.

"We got the same thing, girl. You just got a life growing inside of you. Take this phone; it's getting on my nerves."

Reign looked at the phone and noticed that it was an unknown number. She remembered Pearl calling her from an unknown number and didn't want to deal with her at that moment. Her gut pushed her to answer. "Pearl, I don't have the time today. What's up?"

"Oh no. This isn't, Pearl sweetheart." A deep male voice came through the other end.

"Who is this?" Reign asked as she stopped admiring her belly.

"I know it's been a while, but this is Jameson."

"Jameson?"

"Yes. You don't remember when we spoke when you came to Philly?"

"Yes, I remember. I'm just wondering to what joy do I owe this phone call?"

Jameson cleared his throat. "It's been a couple of months since I last saw you. While I want to get right to what I need from you, I can't do so over the phone. When can you meet me?"

Reign sighed. She forgot all about Jameson asking her to be on his payroll. Rolling her eyes, she responded, "I have an errand to run now and I'm already running late. Could you text me a number where I can contact you when I'm done, and we could discuss where I could meet you?"

"Sure," he simply said and hung up the phone.

Reign threw her phone on top of the vanity and climbed into the shower. As she washed, she thought deeply about her position in the game that she was in. While she wasn't hurting in the money aspect of it, she was now carrying a child and wondered if she should take some time off just until she gave birth. Letting the water beat down her back, she figured she would call Jameson. If she didn't like what he was talking about, she would pull out. Or even yet, add him to the long list of people who are in the dirt with crimson red hearts on their wrists.

Reign was done in ten minutes flat and she rushed into her room to get dressed. She moved as fast as she could to make sure she didn't hear her grandmother's voice rushing her. She grabbed her phone and left her room.

Nana and Jackie were sitting on the couch as she had approached the living room. They were watching the news and it just so happened that they were covering Senaj's kidnapping. They said that he had went to school officials and spoke with them, letting them know that he was okay and about his future plans. They said that they asked Senaj to write a statement about what happened, but he declined, saying that all he wanted was for the press to respect his privacy. All he wanted to do was put his degree to work and become the best pediatrician that he could be. Once they noticed Reign was standing there, they turned the TV off and Nana grabbed her purse.

"You ready?" Nana asked.

"Yes, ma'am. Jackie are you coming?" Reign asked.

"No, not this time. I'm going to help you out around here and clean up and have lunch ready by the time you get back."

"Okay. I appreciate it."

"Any time."

Nana and Reign walked out, got into Reign's Audi and made their way to the doctor.

Nana looked over to Reign and she could tell that she was nervous. "Reign, you don't have to worry about anything. I'm sure that Senaj will accept you having this baby with open arms."

"I don't know about that, Nana. He was so mad last night. I have been nothing but a fuck up this relationship, Nana, and I don't know if I would be able to repair it."

"You don't know that until you speak with him. Today is a new day, so I think that you should try again after this appointment."

Reign sighed, putting her hand on her head. "Nana, I have something to do afterward. I forgot about this guy who was the one who told me that Uncle James wanted me dead. He told me in exchange for that information, he wanted me to work for him. He called me today and brought it back up, and now I have to meet up with him."

It was now Nana's turn to sigh, taking a quick glance at her grandchild. She wanted to tell Reign that she's going to have to relax and worry about this baby, but she knew that Reign was her father's child. She wouldn't rest until she was cold and in the dirt. Instead, Nana said, "I've been meaning to talk to you about that money that James was trying to kill you over."

"What about it?" Reign asked, changing her mood.

"I know where it is."

Up until that point, Reign had lost all hope about finding the money. She folded her hands into her lap. "How long have you known about it?"

"Since before your father passed. It's in a safe at my house. I wanted to give it to you when you showed up, but when you began to tell me all the shit that had been going on with James, I figured that it could wait until the issue with James was handled."

Reign was grateful that her money was somewhere safe. If that money had been anywhere remotely close to anywhere James thought that it could be, she would have been out seven million dollars. Ten minutes later, they arrived at the doctor's office where Reign was prompted to fill out some paperwork.

When Reign finished, Nana brought the paperwork up to the receptionist and took her seat next to Reign. The nervousness was written all over Reign as she sat, twiddling her thumbs. This was her first pregnancy ever and she didn't even know where to begin to think about how she was going to be a mother. Her mind raced as she wondered what her baby would look like. *Would Senaj be happy about the baby?* she thought.

"Nana, what if Senaj isn't happy?" Reign asked. She sat up so straight in her seat that Nana thought that she would bolt straight for the exit.

"You don't have to worry about that right now. I have no doubts that he would be happy."

A nurse came from the back and grabbed a clipboard from the front desk. She briefly looked over the papers as she yelled, "Reign Mills!"

Reign stood up and looked behind her. She noticed that her grandmother didn't get up. "You not coming with me, Nana?"

"Baby, there are somethings that you are gonna have to do by yourself. If I was Senaj then I would be there in a flash. But I am your grandmother and I don't want to see your little coochie."

Reign rolled her eyes and followed the nurse to the back. The nurse checked her vitals, and after she was satisfied, she told her that the doctor would be in with her in a few minutes. As she sat on the table, she took her phone out and sent Senaj a text, letting him know that they would need to meet later in the day. His response was quick and straight to the point. He said that he would be over to her place around six.

The doctor came in just as Reign placed her phone on top of her clothes. "Hello, Ms. Mills. I'm Dr. Patel and I will be your doctor for today. How's everything?" She asked.

Reign looked up at one of the most beautiful women that she'd ever seen in her life. She had skin the color of cinnamon, her eyes were a light green, and her body was shaped something fierce. Her dimples dipped so deeply into her cheeks it made Reign jealous just a little bit. Her hair was up in a messy bun with a few loose strands framing her face.

"Everything is okay, considering this is my first pregnancy and I'm scared to death." Reign spoke with nervousness lacing her voice.

"Trust me, there isn't anything to be scared about. As women, as soon as we push another human out of us, our instincts just kick right in and we do what we've seen our mothers and grandmothers have done," Dr. Patel responded.

Reign felt at ease as her doctor performed her duties. At the end of her exam, Dr. Patel had a nurse wheel in an ultrasound machine. Reign's heart almost leaped out of her chest as she grew with anticipation of hearing her baby's heartbeat.

"Can I find out the sex of the baby?" Reign asked.

"If the baby wants us to know what he or she is, then yes," Dr. Patel stated.

Grabbing the blue gel from the machine, she squeezed some on Reign's stomach, causing Reign to jump a little due to the coldness. The doctor took the wand from the machine and placed it on Reign's stomach. Almost immediately the room was filled with the sounds of her child's heartbeat. Tears fell from her eyes as her heart felt whole. Grabbing her phone, she began to record the sound of the heartbeat.

After a few minutes passed, Dr. Patel spoke. "Baby is growing healthy. Heartbeat is strong. And baby's legs are

closed. Maybe next time the baby's legs are open and hopefully we'll know. I'm going to print out some ultrasounds and
then you can get dressed and, on your way out, make an appointment for three weeks out."

Reign felt on top of the world as she got dressed and awed
over the ultrasounds. She couldn't wait to share the news with
Senaj.

Chapter Six

Jameson's dark brown Stacy Adams leather shoes clicked across the linoleum floor as he held that day's newspaper in his hand. The head story was about James being found dead in an abandoned warehouse and the only evidence that the police had was the heart drawn on his wrist with lipstick. The newspaper reported that James was under investigation and they were close to an indictment. At that current time, they had no leads or suspects and they reported that they would be continuing their search in finding the Lipstick Killah.

With a smirk, Jameson placed the newspaper down on the counter top and moved to the refrigerator to pour himself some orange juice. He had big plans for Reign and he knew that they would both make some good money. All he had to do was have her on board with his plans and they would become a force to be reckoned with. As Jameson sipped his juice, he walked over to his sliding backdoor and looked across his backyard. He squinted and noticed that there was a woman dressed in a colorful summer dress with flat sandals on her feet and her hair was flowing down her back.

Placing his cup on the counter, he slid the door open with one hand while he used his other hand to hold on to the .45 that rested on his hip. Trying his best to stay quiet he inched his over to her with his arm raised and steady, ready to bust his gun at any sudden movement.

"You don't have to creep, Jameson, it's only me," Reign said without even having to turn around to address him.

"How did you hear me?" he asked, walking around to stand in front of her.

"You suck at sneaking up on people. Anyway, you wanted to talk. I'm here to listen."

"How about we go inside? It's pretty hot out here."

Reign looked Jameson up and down and laughed. Of course, he was hot. He was standing in the sun with a three-piece suit on. She didn't feel comfortable going inside but she did so anyway. It was a relief once she went inside. She welcomed the cool air as she closed the sliding door behind her. In case she had to take flight, she left the door slightly ajar and her arms crossed over her torso, just in case she had to reach for her .22 that sat snugly in an extra piece of fabric attached to her dress.

"Talk."

"Your uncle's death is all over the place."

"And?"

Jameson scratched the back of his head as he decided to just leave that topic alone. He began again. "Um... I would like it if you came and worked for me. I'm trying to go places, but I can't get there because there are several people in my way. I need your help."

"Why do you need my help? You can't take them out yourself?"

"Me taking them out isn't the problem. You see, I'm trying to be out here on some Mafia or Cartel type of time and I can't have my name mixed into nothing like that. I like the way you take care of your business. You are in and out, and that's what I need to have done. I can guarantee you that if anything comes even close as to your name being related in anything, then I can assure you that it will get thrown out of the window."

"How can I believe that? I don't know you from a can of paint."

"My grandfather is the Police Commissioner. Come on, Reign, I need your help with this. With each hit, it'll be a sixty-forty split. And—"

"Whoa, whoa, whoa. Who's getting sixty and who's getting forty?" Reign asked, unfolding her arms. She placed her hand on the counter and leaned in toward Jameson.

"Well—"

"My ass! Holla at me when that percentage change. You must remember that I'm the one who puts her life on the line. Keep in mind that I am now pregnant, and it will be that much harder for me to get work done. So, if it ain't eighty-twenty, you could find yourself someone else. Just know that if you do decide to go that route, they won't at all be as great as I am." Reign spoke like a boss before she turned her back and began to walk out the sliding doors.

"Reign, wait. You got it. And congrats on the new edition. But if you're pregnant, wouldn't that get in the way of things?"

"You don't need to know about that. If I take care of what I need to take care of, that's all that you need to worry about. I need to get some things in order. I will contact you in a week. We'll set something up then." Reign winked and left the house through the sliding doors.

Not even a full ten seconds had passed when Jameson walked to the doors and looked out. Reign was nowhere to be found and Jameson could do nothing but smirk. He knew that working with Reign was going to prove worthwhile.

Jameson pulled out his phone and touched the screen a few times. After retrieving the number that he was looking for, he waited for the other person to pick up. "That first case I told you I needed handled, put that together within the next week."

The person responded, "I'm on it."

***

Senaj's heart beat from his chest as he drove to Reign's house. His parents tried everything to stop him from coming but he knew he had to give her the chance to speak her piece.

His parents wouldn't understand, and he regretted yelling at his parents, but he wasn't a child anymore and he had to deal with things his way. Senaj decided on going over to Reign's house. Even though her family didn't know him, they didn't give him any grief, and he knew that he would peacefully be able to talk with Reign. Whereas if he told her to come to his house, his mother would have been lurking around every corner, eavesdropping.

Light rain hit his windshield as Senaj exhaled. It seemed like every time that it rained, there was never anything that came of any good. Senaj's temple ached as the past few days' events tossed around in his head. The meeting with his administrator went surprisingly well. Senaj would be starting his fellowship in a few weeks at one of the best hospitals in New York City. He was happy, but due to the constant whirlwind that was now called his life, he knew that his high wouldn't last long. For there is always something lurking to dim his light.

Senaj parked his car near Reign's garage and sat for a few minutes before he decided to get out and approach the house. The black truck that sat next to his car let him know that Reign's family was still in town. He wanted to meet them but that would have to wait until he spoke with Reign.

"You gonna come in or stand out here in the heat?" Reign spoke, peeking her head out of the door.

Senaj slightly placed a smile on his face and walked up to the door. His tall frame hung over her as she bent her neck back and looked into his eyes, getting lost.

Senaj asked, "How long you knew that I was here?"

"Since you pulled up. You should know that I have camera's all over this place like it's the White House."

They walked inside the house where Senaj briefly looked around the living room for her family. "Where is everybody?"

"In the basement. They knew that we needed to talk, and they wanted to give us our own space. I took the liberty into making dinner, so I hope that you are hungry." Reign stated as she made her way into the kitchen.

Senaj followed Reign as he watched her ass bounce around in her multi-colored sundress. This was Senaj's first time paying attention to Reign's body since he'd been back home, and he not only noticed the glow to her skin but also that her hips widened, and her thighs were a tad bit thicker. Her breasts were fuller, and he couldn't help but to get excited.

"What did you make?" Senaj asked, biting down on his bottom lip. He had to shake the images from his head that he was having. He saw himself throwing Reign onto the table and sliding all nine inches of his thickness inside of her. It had been months since he felt her insides and he couldn't help but want that at the current moment.

"Did you hear what I said?" Reign asked, turning from the stove.

"No, I didn't. I'm sorry, I had something on my mind."

Reign's eyes lowered as she felt bad about all that had gone down. She said, "Look Senaj, I don't know how often I could apologize for what happened. I should have never put you in that position, and every day I beat myself up about it."

"Of course, I accept your apology, but that was the furthest thing from my mind right now. I get that we have to talk about that at some point, but I can't help but to want to bend you over and feel your walls tighten around my dick."

Reign's mouth dropped. "Such language, Doctor. But that is going to have to wait for a little while longer. I promise this kitty misses all that you have to offer. Just wait it out a little longer."

Senaj folded his arms across his chest and rolled his eyes as Reign giggled. From the stove, she placed baked macaroni and cheese, collard greens with smoked turkey necks, baked curried chicken wings, and a pitcher of lemonade on the table. Reign began to put food on their plates, poured their drinks and slowly they began to eat without saying a word. Senaj waited for Reign to speak but the glances that he stole at her told him that she was a nervous wreck. Midway through their meal, Reign reached for her phone that sat on the counter behind her. As Senaj put a forkful of baked macaroni and cheese into his mouth, the sounds coming from Reign's phone stopped him in mid-chew. With tears clouding her eyes, Reign looked up at Senaj with a smile on her face.

"What is that?" Senaj asked as he listened intently at the sound.

Struggling to speak, Reign exhaled and said, "That is your son or daughter's heartbeat."

Senaj forced the macaroni and cheese down his throat as he made his way to the other side of the table where Reign sat, crying happy tears. "I'm gonna be a dad?"

"Yes. I went to the doctor today and they said that I am sixteen weeks. We tried to see if it was a boy or a girl, but the baby had its legs closed. I think the baby did that so that I could tell you first."

Senaj forgot all about the kidnapping, and happiness poured all over his body. He couldn't believe that he was about to be a father and it was going to be with the girl that he was in love with no less. Nothing else mattered to him at that moment except his unborn child. Senaj wasn't one to cry, but in that moment as he hugged Reign and touched her belly, just at his slightest touch, the baby kicked and moved, causing tears to flow from Senaj's eyes. He kissed the top of Reign's forehead.

Senaj placed his lips against her ear and whispered, "Now can I put my pee pee in you? I hear pregnant pussy is the best pussy."

Reign's mouth dropped. "Okay, whoever you've been hanging out with, please stop. They are having a bad influence on the way you talk to me. But yes. Yes, now you can place your enormous pee pee in me."

Reign jumped from the chair she sat in and ran up the stairs to her bedroom. Senaj couldn't help but to chuckle as he chased behind her. By the time he made it upstairs, Reign was fresh out of her sundress and laying on the bed in just her bra and thong. From the doorway, Senaj could see the bulge of his child laying in Reign's stomach. Senaj took his shirt off and his pants as he walked the rest of the way to the bed in his boxers. With one leg bent and the other lying flat on the bed, Reign watched as Senaj made his way up her body. He placed soft kisses on her calves and soon to her inner thighs, causing a giggle to escape from Reign's lips. Using his body to pry her legs open, Senaj used his index finger to pull the cup of her bra down from her tiity and placed her nipple in his mouth.

Their eyes met, and a smile was placed on Reign's face. The feeling that came over her was overwhelming and she couldn't help but to allow the tingling feeling rush all over her body. Reign closed her eyes as Senaj made love to her nipples with his tongue. Slowly he moved his way down her body, placing soft kisses against it. He pushed open her legs with his shoulders and slid his tongue in between her slit. Reign's back arched as she allowed Senaj to devour her clit with more access. Sliding his index and middle finger inside Reign, he expertly hit her g-spot as he made a come here motion. Reign's mouth dropped open as she felt herself getting ready to cum. Senaj knew it just as well and he pulled away just as she was about to release.

"What? Why did you stop?" Reign spoke as her legs shook on top of Senaj's shoulder.

Senaj only smiled as he tapped his two fingers against her clit and got on his knees. Wrapping his arms around her thighs, he pulled her closer to him, until her pussy was sitting right at the tip of his dick. Using one hand, Senaj guided himself into her tightness. His eyes snapped shut as her vagina squeezed tightly around him. It took everything in Senaj to not cum. He had missed this part of Reign so much that he was ready to let loose prematurely. Reign's moans echoed around the room as he slowly moved inside of her. Senaj moved his head to the crook of her neck and deeply inhaled her scent.

"Don't ever leave me again, Reign. I damn near went crazy without you," Senaj said.

"I'm not going anywhere any more. That I can promise." Reign said seriously as she looked into his eyes. She needed him to believe every word that she said.

His lips on hers confirmed that he did. Anything that happened before this night, they knew that it didn't matter. They left it right where it needed to be as they decided silently to themselves, instead of running they would take the time out and talk about whatever issues that they needed to.

***

Three o' clock came fast for Reign and Senaj, and although they were knocked out, the sound of banging woke them from their sleep. Reign jumped from the bed along with Senaj as she fumbled to secure the tie on her robe. As they reached the hallway, Nana, Jackie, and Jamori were strapped and looking down the hallway toward the stairs.

"So, nobody is going to answer the door?" Senaj asked. When no one moved, he began to move toward the door.

Reign stopped him. "Just stay behind me."

"Reign, you not strapped. Let Jamori go first," Jackie stated.

Reign reached into the pocket of her robe and raised a .22. She said, "What you mean? I stay strapped."

Reign placed the gun back into her robe and proceeded to head toward the stairs. The banging got louder. Everyone else followed Reign's lead as they situated themselves in a position to bust if need be.

"Who is it?" Reign called out.

"NYPD. Ma'am, we need you to open the door. It's an important matter," came from the other side of the door.

Moving expertly, Nana grabbed everyone's guns and made her way to stash them. Jackie replaced Reign at the door as she pushed her inside of the living room with Senaj. Jackie took a quick second and made sure that everything was calm before she opened the door.

"Yes, officer. What is the matter?" Jackie asked, folding her arms across her chest as if she was cold, even though there had to be eighty degrees worth of heat blasting into the house.

"Are you Reign Mills? It involves your uncle. May we come in?" The officer asked.

Jackie moved aside as soon as Reign decided to jump up. She said, "I'm Reign Mills. What's wrong with my uncle?"

"I'm Officer Green and this is Officer Hobbs. Your uncle was found wounded in an abandoned building with a gunshot wound to the head. It's a miracle that he is even still alive. There was some damage and the doctors placed him in a coma so that it could help him recover from his injury. The doctors at the hospital contacted us and your name and address were listed as his next of kin. We thought that we would come and break the news to you. We do apologize that it's at this late hour, but we had to make sure that he was out of surgery to at least bring you some good news." Officer Green stated.

The look on Reign's face remained emotionless as she fumed on the inside. "Thank you, officers. What hospital is he in?"

"He is at the Hackensack Meridian Health Jersey Shore University Center in Neptune City, New Jersey. Sorry again to bring you this news so late. We are helping the police in Jersey to find out what happened. If you know or find out anything that would be helpful to this case, please feel free to give me a call at this number." Officer Hobbs passed Reign a card.

Officer Hobbs and Officer Green shook hands with Reign and quickly made their exit. Jackie locked the door behind them and stood at the front window and watched until they backed up away from Reign's house.

"What the fuck? How is he still alive? That bullet should have ended his life! I saw brain matter. Senaj let that thing go better than I would have!" Reign roared.

"Reign, calm down. You don't want to upset the baby," Jamori spoke.

"Jamori, he's still alive! I can't calm down." She paced across the living room floor.

"Reign, we are all shocked at this news. You need to relax because I'll be damned if I'm rushing you to the emergency room tonight." Senaj spoke calmly but firmly.

Reign looked at Senaj and she knew that he wasn't playing. Only he was able to achieve that. Reign stopped pacing and took a seat on the couch.

Nana stood in the corner with a smirk.

"We just need to come up with a plan to finish the job. And not get caught," Jackie spoke as she picked up where Reign left off with pacing.

"How about we just all go back to bed and comeback to the drawing board?" Nana suggested.

"No, Nana. I don't know if I can go back to sleep with this weighing heavy on my mind," Reign said.

"You can, and you will. Senaj, take her upstairs. She hasn't grasped fully that she is carrying precious cargo and she needs to take it easy," Nana stated.

Senaj nodded in agreement and held his hand out for Reign to take it.

"But—"

"But my ass, Reign. Take that man's hand and go get some sleep. End of discussion." Nana placed her arms across her chest.

Reign rolled her eyes as she reluctantly grabbed Senaj's hand. She wasn't so much irritated with her grandmother, but the thought of James surviving that gunshot pissed her off. Once Senaj got Reign upstairs, she attempted to speak, but Senaj hushed her.

"Listen, I get that you are upset, but please, let's just get some rest. I must be at the hospital at ten. I'm exhausted. Please, let's just get some sleep," Senaj said. He placed a kiss on her lips, and as much as it killed her, she submitted to Senaj and climbed inside of the bed with him.

Within minutes she was out like a light. On the other hand, the realization of Senaj shooting another human being set in. He shook with fear of the outcome and hoped like hell this wouldn't back fire.

Mimi

Chapter Seven

"Ma'am, how can you be so sure that this is the right person?" Homicide detective Winslow asked.

"Because she killed my child's father right in front of me," the very pregnant woman stated as she wiped tears from her eyes, which to the detective it seemed real. Little did he know, it was her best performance yet.

"What proof do you have? We can't just go around arresting people without concrete proof of what you're accusing someone of doing. You said her name is Reign Mills. I checked the database and she doesn't even have so much as a parking ticket. Do you know how much chaos this would cause?" Detective Winslow asked. As soon as this lady left his office, everything that she had signed was going into the shredder. He figured that when he got the call, he thought this would move him further in his case, chasing The Lipstick Killah. He was met with a dead end.

"Wouldn't it be enough that I'm telling you that she killed my child's father in front of me? What am I supposed to do?" She cried.

"Okay, ma'am. I'm sorry he's gone. Give me the time and day that it happened, and I will make sure that I drop in for a visit. I have one more question for you."

"Of course."

"Why did you wait so long to come to the police? You wrote on this paper that it happened last year around Thanksgiving."

"She left the state for a while, but I didn't know. By the time I found out, she was back. Now I'm afraid for my life because I think that my child and I are next."

"How do you know this woman?" Detective Winslow asked, flipping through the papers he had on his desk.

"She was my friend before I found her in bed with my boyfriend."

"I-I don't think I got your name, or at least I forgot what it was."

"Pearl." She was done with answering questions, so she grabbed her purse and began to waddle out of the door. She rubbed her stomach and a smirk appeared on her face as she walked out of the police department. She knew that by the time Reign got wind of what she did, and she will deal with the consequences when the time came, but she needed to bring Reign out. Pearl knew that sending the dogs her way and lying about why Reign had an affiliation with Stanley's death was a lie, but desperate times called for desperate measures. Now Reign had no choice but to come to Pearl and hear her out. Pearl just hoped that she would give birth before Reign did come for her.

Pearl didn't realize that she put herself out there to be investigated as well. That's if Winslow decided to take this portion of his case serious. Pearl climbed inside of her car and drove to the nearest McDonald's and got her something to eat. Once she grabbed her food, she drove out to James' house where she had been for the past couple of days, waiting for his return. He told Pearl that while he was gone, she could stay at his house until he got back from handling his business.

Pearl entered the house and looked around. She wondered how her life had come to this. All she wanted was her best friend. She didn't have anyone else to share the joys of motherhood with. Her family disowned her years ago when she had decided against her mother's wishes, when her mother found out her only daughter was sleeping with her Pastor. Pearl thought back to that time in her life as she sat her food on the table.

Pearl was seventeen and a senior in high school. Pearl attended church with her mother every Sunday as usual, and this Sunday she did so without any thought. She wore a knee length black wool knitted DKNY dress with black stockings and black DKNY flat shoes. Her hair hung down her back with a slight bump at the ends. They arrived at the church, got the word, and as they were leaving, Pearl said that she would stay behind to help clean up the church. Pearl's mother didn't think nothing of it because since Pearl was old enough to go places by herself, she would volunteer to stay afterwards to clean up. They said their goodbyes and Pearl continued to clean up.

After an hour and a half, Pearl was done, and she was going to the Pastor's office to let him know that she was on her way out. She knocked on the door and peeked her head in, telling him that she was done. Pearl was just about to stick her head from the door when the Pastor asked for her to come inside of his office. Not knowing how, the conversation went from how proud he was to have been able to see her grown up to Pearl sitting on top of his desk with her legs opened wide like she was getting a pap smear. From that moment, every Sunday, for two years, the Pastor and Pearl met in his office after service to fuck.

The day Pearl's mother caught them just so happened to be the day of her father's death anniversary. Coincidentally, it landed on a Sunday. Pearl, now twenty, stayed after church and cleaned and met with the Pastor. To much of Pearl's surprise, the Pastor was sitting in his chair, ass naked, stroking his large, rock-hard penis. Pearl quickly disrobed and fell to her knees as her lips wrapped around his love stick.

It was when the Pastor put Pearl across his desk with one hand grabbing the back of her neck and his other was pulling at her hair, that Pearl's moans echoed loudly throughout the small office. They both were on the verge of releasing as the door swung open, startling the both of them. Pearl grabbed at her clothes as she watched while anger washed all over her mother. That same day was when Peal moved in with Reign. Quite a few years later, Pearl found out the reason her mother was so angry was because Pearl's mother was also having an affair with the Pastor.

Pearl laughed to herself as she cleaned up her mess. She retreated to the living room and turned the TV on. The news channel came up and the Chief of Police in New Jersey was talking about controlling crime in the city, he had mentioned the Lipstick Killah moving onto their territory, and they found somebody in an abandoned building. He had a heart-shaped lipstick mark on his wrist. One of the reporters asked if the victim was going to make it.

"We have reached out to the NYPD because that's where his ID says that's where he is residing. They are doing what they can to get in touch with his family. He's in recovery as we speak, and there are currently no suspects. The NYPD are doing all they can to locate his family, but we need the public's help. If you know James Mills, please come forward and get in contact with the New Jersey police department at 732-555-2367." The Chief of Police walked off the stage and the news station switched back to the anchors.

Pearl sat on the edge of her seat as she felt a sharp pain shoot across her lower abdomen and lower back. She needed to find out what hospital he was in to go see him. Pearl decided one more time that she would try calling Reign. The phone rang out and she threw the phone into the wall and fell into the couch in frustration.

***

"Have a good day, love. I'll see you when you get home," Reign said as she placed a kiss on Senaj's lips.

He smiled and rubbed her stomach. Senaj didn't want to leave but he knew if he wanted to keep his job he had to go. Reign watched Senaj as he got in the car and pulled away from her house. As soon as she saw his car disappear down the block, she ran into the kitchen where everybody was sitting at the table eating eggs, sausage, grits, and toast.

"Why is everyone sitting around eating?" Reign asked, looking at everybody like they were crazy. She was in fact the one that looked crazy.

"If you don't sit your ass down to eat. You not going to miss nothing. You heard what the police fucking said. He's in a coma." Jamori spoke, chuckling at Reign.

Reign walked over to the table and smacked Jamori across the back of his head. While huffing, she took a seat and grabbed a sausage off the platter. Her mind raced as she thought about how James survived the gunshot. There was brain matter and a bullet hole the size of a quarter.

Jackie watched as Reign racked her brain and said, "You could sit there and stress yourself out about how he lived, or you can just accept the fact that he did make it. We have a plan, and the only thing that you have to do is go to the hospital, play the distraught niece, leave the hospital in tears, and myself, Nana, and Jamori will handle everything else."

Reign's mouth hung open as she looked at each of her family members. She said, with a mouth full of food, "You have got to be kidding me! I can't do nothing but act like I'm sad that this happened to the bastard! I cannot believe ya'll."

"Told ya'll she won't like it." Jamori spoke sarcastically with a sly smirk.

"Jamori, you really are no help. Go find you some little thot to play with," Jackie stated.

"Just like you found Akuchi to play with?" Jamori sneered.

Jackie's mouth opened. "Excuse me!"

"You heard me. It ain't no secret that you are feeling the nigga. Every time that nigga come around, you look at him with googely eyes."

Jackie was speechless while Reign held her stomach, dying with laughter.

Nana dropped the egg skillet into the sink and turned her attention to her grandchildren. "Ya'll are the most childish, grown motherfuckers I know. Reign, you are going to deal with having to take the backseat on this one. Jackie, if you like the man, so what. After you stopped dating that fake ass blood nigga, you've been hating all men. Even if you just get some dick out of it, go for it. Shit, I heard that African's got dicks as big as horses. And Jamori, go get you a thot to play with. When was the last time you played in some pussy?" Nana walked out of the kitchen and left them speechless.

For five minutes, they just looked at each other, dumbfounded. Reign broke the silence by saying, "Jackie, Akuchi?"

Jackie gulped and answered, "I don't know what Jamori is talking about. He's delusional, 'cause it's been months, maybe even years since he's even smelled a pussy."

"Remember your little friend Rose that you would bring to the house before we came out here? Well she was sucking my dick from the back," Jamori stated with a smirk before he threw his toast down on the table and exited.

Reign once again laughed but was quickly stopped when Nana came back with a serious look on her face.

"Let's go. We got a body to catch," she said, and just as fast as she came, she left.

Jackie and Reign looked at each other and left the kitchen to get dressed. Nana instructed for Reign to dress as if it was just another ordinary day. Nana didn't want to give off any suspect vibes to the hospital staff. She just had to throw on a wig and big shades to cover her face mostly from the cameras. If anything was to go down and the police wanted to investigate anything, they would see a red-haired woman walk into that room. Jackie and Jamori wore black while Nana dressed in skintight jean shorts with a white lacey tank top. On her feet were black gladiator sandals.

"Nana, you look like you are going on a date instead of going to kill somebody," Jamori said.

"I'm going into a hospital where there are plenty successful doctors, and I'm hoping to snag me one."

"Ew, Nana!" Jackie exclaimed as she made her way down the stairs.

"Just 'cause I'm old don't mean that I won't drop this thang on somebody," Nana said as she dropped and popped back up again.

"That's ya'll grandmother," Reign said as they left to the car.

"She's yours too," Jackie said.

"Ya'll knew her first though so that don't count. I win."

"If ya'll don't get inside of the damn car right now. Talking about me like I'm not standing right here," Nana said as she grew angry with their bickering. With laughter, they climbed inside of their car and headed to Jersey.

***

They made it to the hospital and briefed Reign on the plan. All she had to do was show her face and play the distraught niece. She thought that they were joking about that and she did everything but drop to the floor and throw a tantrum. Finally, after ten minutes of them convincing her, she put her shades on and straightened her wig, and made her way into the hospital. She hated that she had to use her real name but the fact that there would be a ten-minute gap for the rest of them to get in and do what they had to do, comforted her.

"Excuse me, I'm looking for my uncle. The police told me that he was here." Reign said as she walked up to the nurse's station.

"What's his name?" The nurse asked.

"James Mills."

After the nurse clicked on the keys, she let Reign know that he was on the seventh floor in ICU. The nurse gave Reign a visitor's pass and gave her directions to the elevator. Reign made it to the seventh floor and walked around until she came across his room. She had to stay there for twenty minutes and then leave the room like she couldn't bare seeing him in his condition. Reign walked inside of the hospital room and was elated that he was hooked up to all the machines. Her heart filled with joy as she saw that he couldn't breathe on his own.

James felt her presence and his monitors began to beep erratically. Although he was medically in a coma, he was able to hear her.

Reign moved closer to the bed and looked down into it. A smile came across her face. "You one lucky bastard. Well not for long anyhow. You should have just gone to hell the first time. Now you got the cops knocking on my door." Reign stated as she went into her purse. She took out her lipstick and almost drew her infamous heart on his wrist. She closed it and stood off to the side to let a few more minutes pass by. Once the time was up, Reign walked up to his bed to look as if she was kissing his forehead, but instead she whispered, "Rest in peace," in his ear. She hesitated before she put her head down and raced out of the room. She made it to the parking lot and speed-walked to the car.

It was empty when she had gotten there, so trying the door, she opened it and sat in the driver's seat with the door open. Time seemed to have been moving in slow motion, and instead of twenty minutes going by, it felt like it was hours. She saw her grandmother and cousins making their way back to the car. Placing her feet into the car, she started it and waited for them to get inside comfortably before she pulled away.

"How did it go?" Reign anxiously asked. No one said a word and they kept it that way until Reign's phone began to ring. Pulling to the side of the highway, she looked at the number that was displayed on her screen. It was unfamiliar, but she answered just in case it was an emergency with Senaj.

"Hello." She answered.

"I'm sorry, Ms. Mills. I know that you just left the hospital, but we need you to come back. It's your uncle." The nurse on the line said.

"What is wrong with him?" Reign asked while fake gasping.

"I'm sorry, I can't say over the phone."

Reign raised her voice and said, "What the fuck happened to my uncle? You tell me right now or so help me God, I will make sure that I hold everyone's job in the palms of my hands."

"I'm sorry, Ms. Mills, your uncle was pronounced dead at 11:47 a.m. and we need you to come and identify the body."

Reign spoke, wanting to jump for joy, "Was it the body that I just visited?"

"Yes but—"

"Okay then. I saw the body. Send him to the morgue."

"But—" was the only thing that the nurse was able to get out because Reign hung the phone up.

"He's gone," she stated before she pulled back into traffic. A smile spread across her face.

Mimi

Chapter Eight

Senaj couldn't help but to think about Reign and his child while at work. While he was still able to focus, he moved around with joy in his heart. He needed to tell his close friends that they were going to be uncles and there were drinks to be bought. He had another hour before he left work, so he sent a text to Rasheed and Polite, telling them to meet him at Smalls Jazz Club. He told them that he had some news to them and that they better be on time.

Senaj was wrapping up a patient chart when his attending came to him and told him to follow her. He closed the chart and as he followed Dr. Graham, he placed the chart at the nurse's station and continued his pace. The doctor briefed Senaj on the patient. Three-year-old boy with a fever of 102.3. No known previous medical history. Possibility the child was teething or catching a cold. Dr. Graham let Senaj enter the room first. The child's mother's back was turned to them as she tried to clean the child's nose.

"Dr. Ademyemi, I have to get to another patient. This is a simple case so I'm pretty sure that you could handle this alone," Dr. Graham said as she patted him on his back.

"Of course." Senaj smiled and watched as she walked away. He cleared his throat, announcing his presence. The mother turned around and Senaj was in complete surprise. "Christina?" Senaj asked making sure that he was seeing correctly.

"Oh my God, Senaj! Hey. How have you been?" Christina asked.

"I've been well." He responded shortly as he moved closer to the exam table.

He began to check the child's vitals and talked to him to make him feel comfortable. In the back of his mind, he couldn't help but to wonder why of all people would Christina show up. He could tell that she was off the drugs, only because she was back to looking like herself before they had decided to get into a relationship. Her hips were wide now that she had given birth to her baby boy. Her breast was fuller and her ass a tad bit bigger. Her hair was cut short in a bob and her dimples were just as deep as the day he met her. Once he was done examining the baby, he stepped away and allowed Christina to go to him.

"It looks to me that he has some redness in his ears which is an indication that it's the beginning of an ear infection. I'm going to prescribe him some Amoxicillin. Give it to him twice a day. If he has a fever give him children's Tylenol every six hours. He will have his first dose here. If his fever doesn't go down take him to the emergency room as soon as possible. For his teething, anything cold will sooth the pain. Being that he's a toddler, a teething ring is no longer an option." Senaj chuckled at his last statement.

"Oh please. I am not one of those parents who keep their kids on certain things even after the age limit requirements." Christina spoke, laughing as well.

"He's going to be fine. Here's his prescription," Senaj said, clicking his pen and placed it in his pocket on his shirt.

Senaj was prepared to walk out but Christina stopped him. She said, "Senaj, I know it might be too late, but I want you to know that I do apologize. I was in a fucked-up head space and hanging out with the wrong people. I've been clean for four years now and Mi'Heir has been my biggest blessing. I've hurt so many people while I was abusing drugs, but I know that I've hurt you the most. A part of my recovery, I must recognize that I've hurt people and even if they don't forgive me, I know that apologizing would make me feel better. If I apologize I can forgive myself for putting anyone that I loved in a position to where I've hurt them."

"Christina, you don't have to worry about me forgiving you. I forgave you a long time ago. I'm glad that you have been sober for four years. Don't stress yourself out about anything that you can't control. Everything will be okay."

"Thank you." Christina said with a smile on her face.

Senaj placed his hand under the hand sanitizer dispenser and rubbed his hands together. Holding onto the door handle, Senaj turned around and said, "It was good seeing you Christina. Take care of yourself and little man. Stay on the right path."

"Wait. One more thing."

"What's that?"

Christina placed her son's sneakers on his feet as he slept. She said, "One day, maybe we could get together for lunch. You know maybe catch up."

"I don't think that would be a good idea. I am in a relationship and she's pregnant with my child."

Christina's eyes bulged. "Oh no I didn't mean it in that way. Congratulations. I meant as old friends. That wouldn't hurt, would it?"

Senaj quickly thought about Reign and how she was. He responded, "If you knew my girl, you would know it would be a problem."

Christina shook her head thinking that Reign was jealous. Only because she didn't know anything about Reign, she said, "Okay. But if you happen to change your mind, take my card."

Senaj was reluctant but he took the card anyway. It said that she was the owner of Christina's Beauty Salon. Senaj said that he would think about it and politely walked out of the room. He slid the card in his pocket and finished his work for the day as he thought about desperately needing a drink.

***

Rasheed and Polite were already seated at the bar at Smalls Jazz Club. They had been stressed out when they saw their friend being kidnapped and not being able to do anything about it. When they found out that he was safely home, they felt much better. They were glad that Senaj told them to meet him. Since Senaj had been home, they hadn't seen him. Quite a few thoughts invaded their minds. They thought that Senaj had looked beat up. They didn't know what to expect. When Senaj told them that he had some good news for them, they thought that he was going to tell them that he doesn't fuck with Reign no more. They despised her after they found out that Reign had something to do with Senaj going missing. They wanted to see the good in her, but the kidnapping fucked them up.

"Fellas." They heard coming from behind them. Rasheed and Polite turned around in their seats and was surprised to see Akuchi instead of Senaj.

"Akuchi! When you get your ass out of prison?" Rasheed asked standing up to give Akuchi a pound. Polite followed and did the same thing.

Akuchi chucked. "The day before Senaj's graduation. I was there when everything happened. Not as close as ya'll were but I was there."

"Mmm. I swear that was the happiest and saddest day of our brother's life. All of ours. Every time I think about that day, all that I could remember is mom dukes screaming and crying bloody murder. That shit breaks my heart every day." Polite said emotionally.

Once again, they were interrupted and this time it was by Senaj. He walked up to them loosening his tie. He said, "I get it ya'll. It was a hard day for everybody. We don't have to relive that moment every day. Please let's just leave it alone and let's just drink. There is a need for celebration." Senaj called over the bartender and ordered a round of drinks for himself and his best friends.

Polite was the first person to speak after they had received their beers. He asked, "Are we celebrating the fact that you came to your senses and you are finally leaving Reign's dangerous ass alone."

"Ha! Ha! No. In fact, I'm going to be with Reign until the day that I die. She, herself, has not done anything at all to me. Before ya'll say something about the kidnapping, I got caught up in it, yes, but a nigga is alive and I'm grateful."

"Yeah, yeah." Rasheed and Polite responded in unison causing Akuchi to chuckle.

"Are ya'll drunk already? I'm just trying to deliver some good news fellas. Don't fuck this moment up."

"Aiight our apologies bro." Akuchi said giving Senaj the floor. Even though he knew what the news was, he was still excited to hear the news.

"Okay. I asked ya'll to be here because a couple of days ago I found out that I was going to be a daddy!" Senaj exclaimed.

There was a moment of hesitation between Rasheed and Polite, and then they expressed themselves by saying congratulations. Senaj noticed and wanted to speak on it. He chose not to and decided that he would later. If he was happy that was all that mattered. They continued to drink and celebrate Senaj, currently putting any issues and sly remarks that they had about Senaj and Reign to the side.

"Okay! Guess who I ran into today? Ya'll won't believe this shit 'cause I'm still in disbelief at this shit." Senaj said, laughing, quite drunk.

"Who?" All three asked together.

"Christina," Senaj answered.

"What?" Rasheed responded.

"Who?" Polite asked, clueless.

"Oh, fuck no! Hell to the nah!" Akuchi stated with the most disgust.

"Yup." Senaj said while taking a swig of his beer.

"What the fuck? When? How? I thought you would never see her ass again." Rasheed said laughing as he envisioned a snot-nosed crying Senaj.

"She brought her kid in for a checkup because he wasn't feeling well. She apologized and said that she had been sober for four years. Asked if we could get together for lunch so that we could catch up."

"I'm just meeting Reign, but bro if you are thinking about hitting that broad up, I will kill you myself." Akuchi stated. He experienced the heartbreak worse than Rasheed and Polite did because he called every day to make sure that his head stayed on right.

"Nah. I told her that it wouldn't be a good idea." Senaj said taking a swig of his beer.

Polite interrupted, asking, "Wait, bruh, you said she had a son? Is he yours?"

"Thank God no! He's only three years old."

Akuchi's phone vibrated in his pocket, indicating that he had a text message. He reached inside of his pants pocket and took the phone out. Standing from the bar stool, he gave Rasheed, Polite, and Senaj a pound and told them he would catch them later. There was something important that he needed to handle. Senaj, no too long after Akuchi left, decided to leave. It was his parents' last night in New York and he wanted to spend some time with them before they left. He wanted to give them the news of them being grandparents and hopefully they would be a little bit more receptive to Reign. If only.

Mimi

Chapter Nine

It was a full week that passed since James was declared dead and for the most part, everything went back to normal. Reign took on her first case back in the game with Jameson. As she got dressed, her cousin Jackie came inside her room and watched as Reign struggled with putting on her Kevlar bulletproof vest. When Reign was satisfied with the fit, she exhaled and sat on the bed to put on her calf-high lace-up black combat boots.

"You know there is going to be a point and time where you're going to be too fat to get those boots on." Jackie said with a chuckle.

"And I will still be the baddest bitch with two guns to walk this earth. What do you want?" Reign asked while rolling her eyes and sucking her teeth.

"Nana in there cutting up on the phone with some nigga. Talking about she's been waiting on the day that she could gargle his balls."

Reign held her stomach, busting out laughing. She said, "Yo, Nana is a fucking nut for real."

Jackie shook her head as she said, "You know tonight, she's having Akuchi over so that she could train him?"

Reign stood up, grabbing her holster with her guns in place. "What the fuck you mean? Train him for what?"

"The type of work we do."

"No. Absolutely not. Let Senaj find out and something happens to his brother, he will have my head on a platter. That I am sure of."

"Well you need to talk to her about that. She says that when you get bigger that you won't be able to move around as much. She wants Akuchi to take your place while you get ready to give birth."

"Why can't you do it? You're already trained."

"I don't know."

"Swear to God that old lady gonna pluck my last nerve." Reign stated irritated. Grabbing her small duffel bags, she placed a call to Jamori who was out following her target. He informed her that he was indeed still in the club. She let him know that she was on her way and if he moved, so did Jamori, and to inform her of their movements.

"You on your way out?" Nana called from the living room, halting Reign from opening the door.

"Yes, ma'am. Nana, when I get back, we gonna need to talk about Akuchi."

"There is no need to talk about it. It's set. He came to me and I'm going to give him what he wants."

Reign rolled her eyes and continued out of the door. If her grandmother wasn't going to listen, then she would speak with Akuchi. Climbing into her Audi, she shook her head. There was no way she was going to let Akuchi get thrown into this life. Especially not after he just got out of jail. Reign made her way through the Brooklyn streets as she traveled to the Social Butterfly. Her stomach grumbled as she grew hungry. *Not now, lil' baby. We got some work to do.'* she thought. It was like the baby knew that she was about to do something that she knew she had no business doing.

Reign picked up her phone and dialed Jamori. When he answered she said, "Jamori, are you still in the Social Butterfly?"

"Yeah, why, what's up?"

"I'm on my way but your damn baby cousin thought it would be a good time to want to eat. Can you order me some lemon pepper wings?"

Jamori laughed like Reign knew he would. Reign cut the call short as she heard her other line beeping. Looking at the screen she saw it was her boobie Senaj.

"Hi, Boobie!" Reign squealed into the phone. She hadn't seen Senaj since the day before when he left for work and she missed him.

"What's up, girl?" Senaj responded, sounding tired.

"You sound so tired."

"Oh, believe me I am. I had to make time for my favorite girl though."

"Aww, Boobie."

Senaj chuckled and said, "What are you doing? I think I want that kitty in my face before I have to go to sleep."

"Ooh, I might have to take a rain check on that."

"What? Why?"

"Because I am out on a job."

Senaj paused and collected himself before saying, "You're joking right?"

Reign knew at this moment that she fucked up. She exhaled and said, "No, Senaj, I'm not."

"You're pregnant, Reign! With my child!" Senaj yelled.

"Yeah, you think that I don't know this, Senaj."

"So why the fuck are you putting yourself out there like that?"

"Senaj, look, I am going to have to call you back to discuss this." Reign said as she pulled into a parking space a few doors down from the Social Butterfly. She expected Senaj to at least say bye, but she was greeted by the three beeps indicating that he had hung up. Tears stung at Reign's eyes, but she brushed it off because now was not the time to cry. Reign picked her phone back up and texted Jamori to come out with her wings.

Two minutes later, Jamori emerged from the club and walked towards her car. He climbed in and passed her the wings. "You look irritated." Jamori stated.

"I don't want to talk about it."

Jamori silently nodded and looked out of the tinted window. He was glad that Reign asked him to come with her to do this job. Since Reign popped up, he's wanted to get to know her better. It seemed like he could never get her by herself and now was his chance.

"Reign?" Jamori said.

"Mmm." Reign grunted, devouring her chicken.

"I've been trying to get close to you for almost six months now, but it seems like Nana and Jackie has been hogging you." He stated with a chuckle.

"That's why I wanted you with me. I only had one friend my whole entire life and never had to deal with so much bickering as I do with Nana and Jackie."

"Who you telling? I had to live with that all my life." Jamori laughed.

"I feel bad for you. My deepest apologies are with you."

"No, but for real. How was it for you just being an only child?"

Reign thought about her answer and said, "My dad did everything in his power to make sure that I was never alone. That only made it worse because it reminded me that no amount of material things that he bought, I was an only child. Pearl became my sister but that was never as satisfying as actually having a sibling. To have ya'll around now, for me, is a true blessing."

"We're glad to have you too because all Nana used to talk about was meeting you. She said that she was able to be around you when you were a baby and then she had to move away. My punk ass pops was supposed to bring you around but that never happened. Between him dodging his own seeds and lying about his niece being in foster care, he ain't have the time to sit back and see that his dumb ass was tearing a family apart."

"Well you see where that got him. And he deserved every bit of what he got. What did ya'll do to him anyway?"

"Nana injected arsenic acid into his IV. About five milligrams of it. He most likely was dead before all five milligrams was able to hit his system."

"Nana is a beast. I'm going to need to get some of that stuff." Reign stated with laughter.

"The stories she's told Jackie and I, man I'm telling you, she is a definite beast."

There was silence that filled the car as a group of people spilled out onto the streets. Both Reign's and Jamori's eyes searched the crowd as they looked for Guap. Guap was an up and coming heavy hitter in the streets and he was trying to squeeze his way past Jameson by taking his men down. Jameson didn't want to take Guap down. He didn't mind a little competition but Guap had Jameson's nephew hit and it left him a paraplegic. Reign and Jamori watched as Guap hugged a female with a huge ass that put Pinky the Porn Star to shame. She giggled as Guap grabbed a handful of her hair and stuck his tongue down her throat. He whispered something in her ear and walked off, climbing into a silver Lexus RX 350. Reign threw her unfinished chicken in the backseat as she started the car and pulled into traffic, three cars behind Guap.

Twenty minutes later, they had followed Guap into a quiet neighborhood in Fort Greene, Brooklyn. They kept going past Guap and parked a few houses ahead and watched through their side mirrors as Guap got out of his car and sat on the steps of the building. Reign and Jamori wondered if he knew he was being followed and was just waiting on them to show themselves. As fast as that thought entered their minds, a town car pulled up in front of Guap's building and the same girl who he was hugged up with at the club, exited the car. A smile formed on Guap's face as they embraced, and he took her overnight bag from her. Hand in hand they walked up the stairs together and into the building.

"Should we go in now?" Jamori asked with his trigger finger itching.

"No, let's give it another twenty minutes. By that time, they would have a few drinks as well as smoke or snort or whatever it is that they do. Pass me my wings please." Reign stated.

Jamori laughed as he shook his head. By the time Reign was done, the twenty minutes passed and they were climbing out and heading towards the building.

"Fuck, it's locked." Reign commented as she tried the door handle.

"Lucky you have me." Jamori said. He pulled out some tools from his pocket and began to pick the lock.

"That's the only thing my pops never taught me. I guess he didn't think about me having to actually get inside of someone's house." Reign whispered.

"Boom!" Jamori exclaimed with excitement.

The door opened, and they walked into a hallway. There were two doors on the first floor and stairs that led to the second floor. Jamori took the lead and walked up the stairs. He had his nine with a suppressor in his hand while Reign had her twin rose gold Maxim's in hers. They arrived at the second floor and approached a door that had music playing, just enough for the occupants to enjoy and not disturb anyone else. Jamori listened at the door for a while and then told Reign to back up. Jamori took a few steps back and proceeded to run towards the door, shoulder first. He knocked the hinges off and fell to the floor as Reign, one second later entered, aiming her guns at Guap and his girl. She stepped over her cousin who was working his way to his feet.

"What the fuck?" Guap asked as he watched two individuals that he didn't know come into his spot like they were SWAT.

"Don't move or reach for a motherfucking thing and this will go smoothly. Cuz, tie them up." Reign instructed.

Jamori moved closer to Guap while Reign fixed her attention on the female. Shockingly, the girl looked at Reign without any fear. In fact, with her eyes alone, she was daring Reign to come at her. This caused Reign to challenge her, and with the butt of her gun, she came down hard on her nose, breaking it instantly.

***

It was after midnight when Akuchi had made it to Reign's house. He was dressed, ready to train with her grandmother. As he climbed out of the car, Nana was at the door waiting for him. She had a smile placed on her face as he walked up the stairs and she greeted him with a hug. They entered the house and the first thing that Akuchi noticed was that the coffee table was out of the living room and two yoga mats were on the floor. Jackie was standing over one, dressed in black yoga pants and a pink sports bra and black socks.

"What's going on?" Akuchi asked, looking from Jackie to Nana.

"Yoga is a group of physical, mental, and spiritual disciplines. You need to learn this before I could teach you anything. There are times where you need to think about your actions before you do it and I'm pretty sure that being in prison you haven't learned that." Nana stated.

"I've had to practice a lot of discipline being in prison; if I didn't want to be stuck with another murder charge." Akuchi chuckled.

"Well this will teach you another type of discipline. I will leave you two alone." Nana smiled at the both and walked out of the room.

Akuchi walked further into the room and began to take his shoes and pants off. He felt vulnerable being that he now stood in tight briefs that showed just where his penis began and ended. Jackie's eyes wandered along his body as he walked over to the extra yoga mat.

"I'm going to do yoga positions and I want you to watch me and try to do the same exact ones as best as you can. It'll be a little hard at first, but as we go along, it'll get easier. Also, you need to keep your mind clear. It won't work if you don't." Jackie stated. She looked at Akuchi who nodded.

Jackie stood with her legs closed together and then she closed her eyes. She sat down as if she was going to sit Indian style, but instead she made her feet touch and her knees were touching the ground. Her back was straight, and she appeared to be taking deep breaths. Akuchi followed suit and took Jackie's advice about clearing his mind.

Several positions and an hour later, they finished their poses and were laying on their yoga mats. It had been so long since Akuchi had felt this calm and he was feeling great. It was quiet between the two until Jackie asked if he wanted some water. He agreed, and Jackie sprang up and got them some water. When she came back, Akuchi was sitting up against the couch.

"Thank you." Akuchi responded when she passed him the water bottle.

"You know Reign doesn't like the fact that you are doing this." Jackie said sitting on the couch next to him.

"For what?"

"She figures that if Senaj finds out he'll blame her."

"Senaj doesn't need to find out. Simple solution. I will speak with Reign about it. At the end of the day, I'm grown, and I need money fast to be able to take care of my family. I dropped the ball by going to prison and now that I'm out, I need to do what I got to do fast."

"I get what you're saying. Why not just go get a job?" Jackie asked.

Akuchi chuckled and sat on the couch next to her. The heat coming from Akuchi caused heat and moisture to gather between Jackie's legs. She crossed them to try and ease the throbbing in between her legs.

"A nigga fresh from jail with a felony isn't getting a job nowhere fast that pays good money."

"Not true. There are a lot of companies who hire felons upon release."

"Please enlighten me because the amount of applications that I've put in that asked for criminal history has yet to give me a call back."

Jackie looked at Akuchi and said, "With any job, they take almost up to a week to get back to you. But for your information, in New York City alone there are hundreds. American Airlines, Deer Park Spring Water, FedEx, United Airlines, and the list goes on. It's not just fast food restaurants that hire felons anymore."

"Without any job history?" Akuchi asked skeptically.

"I mean it'll be harder to obtain a job without any previous history but it's possible. Many black men think that after they've been in prison for years that going to the streets is the only resort. I know that you weren't a street nigga before you went to prison so there is absolutely no reason as to why you need to be one now. Getting money the fast way isn't the best

93

way. Akuchi, you don't have to do it this way." Jackie spoke with sincerity in her voice.

Akuchi was flattered that she was trying to make him feel better and to see that there was another way. His mind was set though. The faster he went through this training, the faster he could make money.

"Let me tell you something. Me not being a street nigga before I went to prison is an understatement. Senaj doesn't know because I shielded my baby brother from that life. I wanted something more for him and I am so glad that he chose the path that he did. This time that I did was a mistake on my part. I got caught and lied to my family and assured them that it was self-defense. That wasn't my first body I caught. I know how to kill but my thing is the discipline of it all. I was ruthless when I was a young nigga, Jackie. Everyone has skeletons in their closets and I am one of them that's neck deep in it."

Jackie was blown away by his confession and was rendered speechless. He was always about that life and knew that what she had took the time to say went in one ear and out of the other.

"Well—" She began.

"You don't have to say anything else. My mind is made up. Jackie, once I set my eyes on something, that's it. I'm going in."

Jackie stared at Akuchi as his body gleamed with sweat. She thought of something to change the subject, so she said, "I think Reign got some of Senaj's clothes if you would like to take a shower. And of course, you could make yourself comfy on the couch until tomorrow."

"It's okay. I have a spare set of clothes in the trunk."

"Okay. Good. You could use the shower down here. While you do that I'm going to find out where Nana snuck off to." She smiled before she walked away and up the stairs.

Akuchi couldn't help but to smile to himself as he walked out of the house to retrieve his clothes. Once back inside he made his way to the downstairs bathroom to climb inside of the shower. Although Jackie and Akuchi never spoke about it or took any action, he felt the energy between them, and just because he's been away for years, he knew the signs of a female wanting him.

Jackie managed to take her shower that she needed to cool her hot ass down. When she had gotten out, she rubbed coconut oil all over her body and dressed in booty shorts and a tank top. She turned off her bedroom light and turned on her nightstand lamp. She grabbed the book that she was reading and dived right inside. Jackie had gotten so caught up in her book that she didn't hear the knocking on the door until it got louder.

"Come in." She called as she never took her eyes from her book.

"You got any lotion?" Akuchi asked.

At hearing his voice, she looked up and gasped as she watched water drip down his chest and arms. He had a towel wrapped around his waist and she had to do a double take at his print.

"Damn, Nana was right." Jackie said out loud to herself. At least she thought so.

"Excuse me?" Akuchi said shocked but trying to hold back his blush.

"Nothing. I don't have any lotion, I just got coconut oil. Is that okay?" Jackie asked, getting out of her bed.

It was Akuchi's turn to gaze at her body and he knew that her previous outfit didn't do her body any justice. "Yeah, that's fine." He watched Jackie grab the coconut oil from her dresser. Akuchi decided that now he would shoot his shot and see how far he could go with Jackie. Before Jackie moved away from her dresser, he walked up behind Jackie and just stood behind her. He felt her body stiffen and her breathing got heavy. "Why you be looking at me like that?" Akuchi asked, playing with her.

"Like what?"

"Like you want to eat me."

Jackie got herself together and said, "Boy, bye! Don't nobody want to eat you."

Akuchi stared at Jackie in the mirror until she finally looked up at him. For a few moments they stared at each other until Akuchi ran his hand up her stomach and up to her neck. He wrapped his fingers around her neck and watched as she closed her eyes and bit her bottom lip. A smirk appeared on his face as his dick came alive at her reaction.

Hooking his finger into the lace on her shorts, he pulled, completely destroying her shorts all in one motion. Jackie realized what was going on and she turned around, ready to go off on Akuchi but was met with him picking her up. He threw her legs over his shoulders and was face to face with her pussy. Her eyes bulged from their sockets as she watched him watch her. Whatever she was going to say went down the drain and she basically dared Akuchi to do what he was doing.

Accepting the challenge, Akuchi palmed both of Jackie's ass cheeks and pushed her pussy directly into his face. His tongue expertly parted her lips as it found its way to her throbbing clit. Flicking his tongue across her clit and kissing it like it was her lips on her face, almost made Jackie pass out for the overwhelming feeling of pleasure.

"Akuchi, stop. Mmmm," Jackie moaned.

"Nah. You was walking around here eyeing me like you wanted it. I'm giving it to you, and now you want me to stop." He responded into licks of her pussy.

Jackie grabbed the back of Akuchi's head, scared that she was going to fall. She really didn't want him to stop, and if he wasn't willing to, she was going to make the best of this moment. Jackie rotated her hips as she felt Akuchi smile against her pussy. Moments later, she felt herself ready to cum. Akuchi's tongue moved faster against her clit, making it his goal to make her cum. His dick pulsated as he anticipated getting up in her guts. Jackie's legs beginning to shake was his indication that he did a job well done. He let her down on the bed once she was able to stop shaking. Akuchi kissed her stomach up to her breast as he lifted her shirt along the way.

"Do you think that this is a good idea?" Jackie asked looking down at Akuchi, placing her hand on the back of his head.

"I don't care of its right or wrong. Everybody is going to have an opinion on something, but the question is you're grown, are you going to let other people decide what is right or wrong for you?" He asked looking in her eyes.

"No but—"

"No buts, Jackie. Worry about what you think. Now where are the condoms?" Akuchi asked.

Jackie's mind wandered for a few minutes until Akuchi's tongue was wrapped around her nipple. She made up her mind quickly and got up to get one. Smiles adorned their faces as they went at each other like lions.

***

Reign walked around Guap and his female companion, waiting for a return call from Jameson. Jameson wanted to speak to Guap before Reign was to kill him and Reign was irritated to the max. This is not how she worked, and she was going to speak with him to let him know that if she doesn't get in and out on the next case, he could forget about her doing any more work for him.

"Man, what ya'll niggas want?" Guap asked.

"Nothing. We just waiting for a call." Jamori answered.

"If you were here for the drugs, I don't have none here. I got some money and you could keep that if you let us go."

"Babe, they not going to let us go. Whether you give them money or not. And if they do let us go by the grace of God, I will beat the bitch ass until that baby she trying to hide, drops from her weak ass pussy." Guap's girl said, causing Reign to stop pacing.

Reign looked at Jamori who threw his hands up. Her gaze went to Guap who had a smile on his face. Finally, Reign looked at her and watched the fire dance in her eyes. "Little girl, you really trying the little patience that I have left. Now shut your fucking mouth because you would not win in a one on one. The next thing that comes from your mouth is going to land you with a bullet to your head."

"Take me out of these zip ties and I will kick your ass!"

Within seconds, Reign had slit her throat and punctured her heart with a six-inch knife. Guap's mouth dropped open and watched as his girl bled to death. He didn't even find out that she was pregnant with his child. Reign's ringing phone brought everyone back to reality and Reign answered.

"Place me on speaker phone." Jameson ordered. Reign did what he said, and Jameson continued to talk. "You know, Guap, I was down for some competition but I'm sure that you could imagine how devastated I was when you left my nephew a paraplegic."

"Nigga, your nephew? I don't even know who your nephew is?" Guap said. His face registered deep thought.

"Nigga, you know who Raheem is. The only nigga that was out there getting that chicken! You left him confined to a wheelchair for the rest of his life!" Jameson yelled.

Guap acted like he didn't know what Jameson was talking about and as they went back and forth, Jamori stood up from the chair that he was sitting in and showed her the screen on his phone. It was a message from Nana saying that she needed them at the house ASAP. Reign, who was pissed for Jameson prolonging the situation, cut their conversation short as she raised her hand and aimed the gun to his head. Guap looked at her as if he dared her to shoot, and she did. One bullet right between the eyes. For good measures, she grabbed the knife from Guap's girlfriend's chest and stabbed him in the stomach, pulling it upward. She watched as his guts spilled out and between his legs onto the floor. Blood splattered on her shoes and a smile crept onto her face. Reaching into her pants pocket, she produced her Christian Louboutin lipstick, placed her signature heart on his wrists and they walked out of the apartment.

"What's your story with the lipstick?" Jamori asked as they descended the stairs.

"Every assassin has a calling card. Some are more drastic than others but mine is simple. The heart is because I gave a man my heart years ago and he broke it into pieces. The heart was only supposed to stick with Josiah because a piece of my heart died with him, but it just kind of stuck with me."

They reached outside, walked to the car and made their way home. The ride was silent as Reign drove. Both wondered what could be so wrong at home that they had to rush. What was brewing on the home front would be nothing that Reign could ever prepare for.

Mimi

Chapter Ten

Silence filled the living room as Nana, Jackie, Akuchi, and Senaj sat watching each other. Senaj was fuming on the inside as he waited a full hour after speaking with Reign to make his way to her house. When he arrived, he knew that the chances of seeing her car in the driveway was slim to none. His nostrils flared as he walked into the house using his key. Upon entering, he checked the downstairs in hopes of finding Reign but came up empty handed. He headed to the stairs and his heart dropped at the familiar sounds of a woman being pleasured. He took the stairs two at a time and immediately headed to Reign's room. When he opened the door, he realized it was empty, but the sounds continued. Leaving Reign's room, he moved to the door that held the noise behind it. Without thought, he barged inside of the room. For sure his heart dropped to his ass and he just knew that Reign was lying about her going out to kill tonight. She was too busy getting dick from the next nigga!

"Arrrggghhh!" Senaj yelled from the pain that was deep in his soul. All he saw was red as he ran full speed at the dude that was on top of his woman. Punch after punch he was giving it to dude until Nana came running inside of the room.

"Senaj, get off your brother!" Nana yelled. He heard her, but it didn't register to him what she was saying.

Jackie managed to throw a T-shirt over her body before she walked up to Senaj and managed to use her index and middle finger to hit him in a pressure point in his neck. Senaj rolled off Akuchi holding his neck as he looked up. Looking back at him was Nana, Jackie, and Akuchi with his dick swinging like a pendulum in his face.

"Can you put your dick away?" Senaj managed to say.

Nana looked down at Akuchi's dick and a smile crossed her lips. She turned to Jackie and said, "I told you so. I hope he worked that pussy out too."

"Nana!" Jackie exclaimed.

Akuchi picked his towel up from off the floor, wrapped it around his waist and walked out of the room in search for some basketball shorts. Nana stayed with Senaj to help him up while Jackie went to make sure that Akuchi wasn't bleeding or hurt.

"I'm going to text Jamori and tell him to get Reign home." Nana stated.

"Thank you, Nana."

"Go check on your brother."

Senaj followed Nana out of the room and went downstairs to look for his brother to apologize. Senaj found Jackie and Akuchi in the downstairs bathroom laughing so he decided to wait inside of the living room. His mind raced with thoughts as he tried to call Reign. His call went to voicemail and with discouragement, he hung up without leaving a message. Five minutes later, Nana, Akuchi, and Jackie joined Senaj in the living room.

"My bad, Chi. My mind was fucked up. I thought somebody was giving it to Reign." Senaj admitted while laughing.

"Don't worry about it, bro. Just know you won't ever be able to kick my ass like that again." Akuchi responded.

Nana butted in and said, "Reign and Jamori will be here in a few but before they get here, I got word that someone tipped off a homicide detective about Reign being pinned as the Lipstick Killah."

At the news, the room was silent. As Jackie was about to say something, car headlights came through the curtain and a car slid into the driveway. Nana moved quickly towards the window and confirmed that it was Reign and Jamori. Nana moved from the window and took a seat on the love seat with Senaj as they waited for their entrance.

Jamori entered the living room first and looked at everyone. Something heavy must have happened because everyone had a solemn look on their faces. Reign came inside and immediately took off the Kevlar vest. She stood in the middle of the living room with just her bra and jeans.

"You had that shit on constricting my child?" Senaj seethed.

"Senaj, please. We can talk about that later. I will explain everything to you."

"Ain't no later. Why the fuck are you still doing this while you pregnant? I disliked it when you weren't pregnant but you not only putting yourself in harm's way, you're putting your child, my child in harm's way! You need to leave this shit alone until you have this baby!"

Reign spoke in a calm tone although Senaj had aggravated her to her core. She said, "Senaj, nothing is going to happen to myself or our child. If I didn't make sure that I was careful before, I'm making sure like hell now that I am careful. This is me, Senaj, and I thought that you accepted that."

"That was before I knew you were pregnant and going to continue this! Help me make sense of this, Reign!" Senaj shouted. He leaped up from the couch and walked into the kitchen where he knew he would find a bottle of D'usse. He rarely would drink alcohol, but this situation caused him to swallow down two shots. He entered the living room with another in his hand.

"You need to lower your voice. I am not yelling at you so please give me the same respect." Reign stated as she eyed Senaj.

"Oh, I'm gonna shut my mouth entirely. Nana, you have the floor." Senaj said as he threw his drink back.

Akuchi shook his head. He knew if his brother kept drinking, it wouldn't turn out good. He stood up and took the glass from a protesting Senaj.

Reign looked from Senaj to her grandmother. She said, "Nana, what is it?"

Nana exhaled and said, "Baby, someone tipped off a homicide detective and told them that you were the Lipstick Killah."

"What? How? Nobody close to me would do that to me. Ya'll the only ones that know." Reign stated. She looked around at everyone and her eyes landed on Senaj.

"What are you looking at me for?" Senaj slurred.

"It was you, wasn't it? You the only one that has an issue with me still doing this, so you went to the motherfucking pigs!" Reign yelled at Senaj. With lighting speed, she bolted right at Senaj. She was able to punch him square in the jaw before Jackie jumped up and restrained her. All the while she spewed curse words unimaginable Senaj's way.

Senaj tapped under his nose to check if he was bleeding. For sure there was blood on his fingertips. He never thought in a million years that their relationship would come to this. "I can't believe you would think that I would actually do something like this. This is just like the incident with Pearl. You didn't let me explain myself, and this right here I don't have to explain because I didn't do it! I'm out of here."

"Bro, let me put my things on and I'll take you home. You've been drinking." Akuchi stated.

"I'm good." Senaj responded and began to walk towards the door.

Akuchi followed him and grabbed his arm. "I don't care how good you think you are. I'm not letting you leave this crib drunk and giving a reason for one of these racist ass cops to fuck with you."

Senaj snatched his arm away from his brother and said, "I'll be in my car."

Akuchi went back into the living room where Jackie was consoling a hysterical Reign, Nana stood by the dining room door frame, and Jamori had his mouth cocked open wide, knocked out cold. Akuchi grabbed his shirt from the room that was downstairs and put his shoes on.

By that time, Reign had stopped crying. She looked directly at him. "Tell him that I apologize for accusing him and putting my hands on him. Tell him that I will contact him when I'm done handling this situation."

"I got you." Akuchi simply stated as he walked out of the house and to a waiting Senaj.

The ride back to Senaj's place was filled with silence as Senaj tried to wrap his thoughts around what happened. Akuchi wanted to tell him that he was training to takeover for Reign but now was not a good time.

"Bro, what could I be doing wrong?" Senaj asked exhaling.

"You not doing anything wrong, bro. She's just stuck in her ways and doing things her own way. She's not used to having someone by her side."

"Bro, that's no excuse. We've been together for almost a year. She should know by now that that's not the type of shit I'm on."

"You and I know that. You told me before she had been out of the dating game for quite some years. Just be patient with her."

Senaj looked at Akuchi and said, "She put her hands on me, Akuchi. I don't know how much patience I'm supposed to have. I love that woman, but I'll be damned if she feels comfortable to put her hands on me."

"Bro, what you gonna do? Put your hands on her? You know that ain't—"

Senaj interrupted Akuchi. "You know damn well I am not going to put my hands on her. I'm not a gangster but I'm not some punk bitch abuser neither."

"Just give her some time, bro. She's going to come around. Plus, she's pregnant, her hormones are all out of whack. Oh, and she told me to tell you that she apologizes for accusing you and putting her hands on you."

The rest of the ride was silent. The shots that Senaj took finally kicked in and all he wanted was to get something in his stomach and go to bed. It was approaching two o' clock in the morning and he needed to get this rest for work. Akuchi pulled up to Senaj's house and they exited the car.

"I'm gonna catch a cab back to Reign's to see if we could figure this shit out." Akuchi said taking his phone out of his pocket.

"Liar. You want to finish what you started with Jackie. It's cool, bro." Senaj started walking into his kitchen to make a sandwich.

Akuchi chuckled. "I'm gonna check on you tomorrow, bro."

Akuchi walked outside and noticed that there was a black 1985 two-door coupe with tints, idling at the curb. He stood in front of Senaj's building and called Jackie instead of a cab. He told her to grab his keys and drive his car to Senaj's house. Akuchi hated that he didn't have any protection on him because he wouldn't know what to do if these people in this car started shooting in his direction. He wasn't scared but, in this situation, he was definitely running as soon as the window rolled down.

It took Jackie twenty minutes to arrive, and by that time the car had disappeared, but he managed to memorize the license plate number. When Jackie pulled up he jogged to the car and climbed in.

"Where is the car?" She asked looking up and down the street.

"It left about ten minutes ago. I got the plate number though."

"Aiight. Nana got some people who could run the plates. Will Senaj be good? Reign will kill me if something happens to him." She asked before pulling off.

Akuchi thought for a second. The occupants of the car looked like they were just scoping things out but he wasn't for certain. Akuchi sighed and took his phone from his pocket. "Yo, bro, I need you to come downstairs." Akuchi said once Senaj picked up.

"For what? I just got in bed. I thought you left already."

"I called Jackie to come get me. Grab your work clothes for tomorrow. You're going to a hotel."

"What?"

"Bro, just do what I said. You could fight me about it tomorrow."

"Ugh, alright. I'll be down soon." Senaj hung up the phone.

Akuchi looked at Jackie as she sat biting her nails. He reached over and moved her hand from her mouth.

"What?" Jackie asked.

"Why are you biting your nails for? That's a nasty habit to have."

"Just a little nervous that's all."

"About what?"

"Your brother caught us. He had a few drinks, he's gonna say something."

"He's not. Trust me. Catching us is the furthest thing from his mind."

"Oh, here he comes. Drive him in his car and I'll follow." Jackie said.

Akuchi got out of the car and went to meet Senaj by his car. Jackie exhaled as she realized she was holding her breath. She just knew Senaj was going to make his way to the car and question her. As Akuchi pulled off, so did Jackie.

***

Reign sat on the couch after Jackie left and thought about what happened. She knew she was wrong for putting her hands on Senaj but at that moment, in her mind, it was only right to accuse him. She figured that he was scared about shooting James, so he must have gone to the police. At least that's what she thought. Of course, her instinct was to feel bad afterward. If she had any notion that Senaj was a snitch, she wouldn't have gotten pregnant by him. Hell, she would have been bodied him.

"Don't beat yourself up about it. We'll get to the bottom of this." Nana said handing Reign a warm cup. She took a seat on the couch next to Reign and rubbed her legs.

"Nana, I put my hands on him. What was I thinking?"

"Yeah, you were fucked up for that. Don't you think that I would have found out sooner if he was the one snitching? Reign, I've only been around ya'll for such a short period of time, but I can tell that he loves you something serious."

"I know which is why I feel like shit."

"You know what? I think that it's that ole friend of yours. The one that Senaj mentioned."

"Pearl?" Reign asked while sipping her tea.

"Yes."

"She wouldn't do that. We may not be on speaking terms right now but Pearl ain't built like that."

Nana cleared her throat and said, "How could you blame the man that you're in love with? You're carrying that man's baby, but you don't think a chick that you were once close to could have done this? Ain't this bitch the same chick who lied about what happened between her and Senaj?"

"Yes."

"So why wouldn't you think that she did this shit? Every female that has a best friend, close associate, or a regular associate, that's a female, there is always a jealous snake lurking. I'm gonna let that sink in. I'm heading to bed."

Just as Nana got up from the couch, Akuchi and Jackie came busting through the door. After the door was locked, they walked into the living room.

"What's up?" Reign asked looking back and forth between Chi and Jackie.

"After I dropped Senaj off and made sure that he was good, I went downstairs and there was this Oldsmobile two-door coupe just sitting out front of his building. They didn't leave until ten minutes before Jackie arrived. I got the plate number. It could be nothing or it could be something." Akuchi spoke.

"Where is Senaj?" Reign asked.

"He's fine. We took him to a hotel."

"Could you see any of the occupants?" Nana asked.

"No. The tint was so dark it looked like it was just black paint."

"What's the plate number?" Nana asked grabbing a notepad from the TV mantel.

"HYZ400."

"We should know who that belongs to by morning. Everybody get some rest. Reign, think about what I said." Nana disappeared to her room, leaving Reign, Akuchi, and Jackie in the living room in silence.

Reign looked at her cousin and her boyfriend's brother while rubbing her stomach. She squinted and said, "Ya'll fucked didn't ya'll?"

"What?" Jackie screeched.

Akuchi couldn't say nothing, he just smirked.

"Ooh ya'll nasty!" Reign yelled as she ran up the stairs and to her room. She laughed at herself as she began to strip out of her clothes to get in the shower. Reign thought back to what her grandmother said, and she knew that she was right. She hated to admit it, but Pearl had to go, before Pearl single handedly fucked up everything that she had worked so hard for. *I think a final visit to my dear friend is in order*, Reign thought with an evil smirk on her face. Pearl wanted to play with fire, Reign was going to show her how bad it burned.

Chapter Eleven

Senaj sat in front of 1220 Myrtle Avenue as he did every day on his lunch break for a week. He constantly battled himself and asked why was he there. But yet and still he made the drive. Today though, he was going to get out and go inside. Getting out of his car, he walked across the street to the establishment and walked inside. The ding dong of the door being open drew all attention towards him.

"Welcome to Christina's. Is there something that I could do for you today?" The chipper receptionist asked.

Senaj looked around nervously and realized that the attention was still on him. Clearing his throat, he said, "Is Christina in?"

"She is. Do you have an appointment?"

"I don't but I'm pretty sure if you asked her to come out here, the appointment wouldn't matter." Senaj smiled his chipped tooth charming smile.

The receptionist smiled and picked up the phone. She stuttered, "Umm, Christina, the-there's a gentleman here to see you. No, he doesn't have an appointment. He didn't tell me his name but said that if you came out, you wouldn't mind him not having an appointment. Okay." Hanging up the phone, she looked at Senaj and said, "She said to have a seat. While you wait, would you like anything to drink?"

"Bottled water please." Senaj said.

The receptionist passed Senaj a bottled water and he walked away from the desk. As he took his seat, he looked around the salon and was impressed. Everything was white. The floors, the chairs, the shampooing station, even the frames on the wall were white. He felt like he was in God's waiting room with a bunch of cackling women.

A full minute passed and Senaj started to second guess himself. He even thought about making a break for the door. Shit, he was just about to stand up when he saw Christina emerge from the back. She was dressed in a yellow sundress and she wore her hair in beach curls with a yellow flower on the side. Her face was fresh from makeup but her mink lashes were placed with perfection. On her feet, she wore opened-toed brown chunky heels. Her smile was infectious and Senaj couldn't help but smile when he saw hers.

"Senaj. To what do I owe the pleasure?" Christina asked.

"I was in the neighborhood and decided to come in and see how the salon was."

"Everybody is watching because I don't have many men coming in here asking for me. Let's go to my office."

The little voice in Senaj's head told him not to but he went anyway. He peeped quite a few women smile their way. He put his head down and followed Christina to her office.

When he walked into her office, he was expecting to see it decorated in white as well, but to his surprise it was decorated in earth tones and on the wall, there was a huge framed picture of her and her son Mi'Heir, cheesing away. They took their seats— her behind her desk and Senaj in the front.

"Don't bullshit me, Senaj. You weren't just in the neighborhood. I've watched you sit across the street for a week and not come in. So, what's up? You going to tell me what's the deal?" Christina asked, eyeing Senaj.

Senaj exhaled and said, "To be honest, I don't know what I'm doing here."

"Is everything okay with you and your girl?"

"Again, I don't know."

"You seemed as if ya'll were the happiest couple alive when I saw you. What major could have happened from then until now?"

"A lot. Me and Reign are from two different world's; it's likely for us to not have the best of times and then there are times where everything is great."

"So, you need someone to listen?"

Senaj finally realized that he wasn't looking at Christina so when he answered, he made sure to look at her. "Maybe to have someone to see my side."

"Well let's hear it."

Senaj placed his arms on the desk in front of him and battled himself if he wanted to lay all his burdens on her. Against his better judgment, he spilled the beans. Of course, leaving out anything that would suggest that Reign was a hired killer. As Senaj spoke he realized that there wasn't much to tell. Except that he's barely spoken to her in the last week, and due to a "disagreement", she was comfortable to put her hands on him.

"All I can tell you, Senaj, is to give her some time. You say she's pregnant, so her hormones are all over the place. Women are delicate at this time. Just be patient."

"You know what? You're right. Thank you."

"Any time."

"I have to get back to work. Sorry to disturb you from you running your own business and all."

Christina blushed and tried to hide it by laughing. She said, "Oh please. I just be in here 'cause Mi'Heir be at daycare and if I stay home, I will be bored out of my mind."

Senaj stood up and looked down at Christina. "It was nice seeing you, Christina. You take good care of yourself."

"You are saying that like we won't run across one another again."

"Truth of the matter is that we won't." With that, Senaj disappeared out of her office and the salon. He went back to work beating himself up and knowing that he couldn't do that type of thing ever again.

When Senaj left Christina's office, she couldn't help but to reminisce on the good times. A smile crept on her face as she remembered what every one of his kisses felt and tasted like. They were always a hint of mintiness behind his kisses. Reminiscing even further, she thought about all the sex they used to have. She had yet to find someone that was both as tender and aggressive as Senaj.

"I'm gonna get that old thing back one way or another," she said out loud. A sneaky smirk donned her face.

***

Reign lay in bed as she thought about all that had happened within the last two weeks. She didn't know who she should trust. The one person that she was close to was dropping dimes on her left and right. She couldn't help but to feel like it was just her against the world. Everything in her life was just starting to feel complete. Now she's second guessing herself.

"Life was much simpler when I was alone." She said to herself.

Going on twelve in the afternoon, Reign decided that she was going to get up and start getting herself together for her doctor's appointment. She was finally going to find out what she was having, and she hoped that Senaj showed up. They hadn't seen other in a week and it was killing her because she knew it was her fault. Akuchi told her that he told Senaj that she apologized but she felt the need for it to come from her mouth.

After Reign had showered, she oiled her body with coconut oil. She dressed in ripped light blue jean shorts, and a red short sleeve shirt that had a zig-zag string design on the back. She placed her feet in black Michael Kors thong sandals. Her hair, since being pregnant, had grown a tremendous amount and was so thick and full that she had begun to wear her own hair out. Today she placed it in two cornrows and placed gold hair accessories on her braids. She put in her gold hoop earrings and gave herself a onceover in the mirror.

"To be five months pregnant, I look damn good." She said smiling to herself. Spraying on some Cashmere Jasmine perfume, she grabbed her purse and made her way out of the door. Surprisingly, after she had gotten dressed, she was in a better mood and she couldn't help but to feel excited to see her man. That's even if she was able to still call him that.

It was a bit chilly on this wonderful July day. Reign rode with the windows down, playing Keyshia Cole's album *The Way It Is*. Within half an hour, she was arriving at her doctor's office and putting her car in park. Grabbing the door handle, she felt the door being opened, and within a millisecond, she had a .22 under Senaj's chin.

"Chill, it's just me." He said with his smooth, deep voice.

"Oh my God! I'm so sorry, babe." Reign said putting her .22 back it's hiding spot. Grabbing her purse, she grabbed Senaj's extended hand and climbed out of her car.

"If you need to pull a gun out in broad daylight as you just did, maybe be more aware of your surroundings." Senaj calmly stated as he placed his arm on the small of her back.

"Look at you trying to give me advice. I admit I was a little off guard. I'm in a good mood and I let my guards down just a tad." Reign responded.

Senaj stepped in front of her and opened the door. They walked in and signed in. The place was packed with mothers from different walks of life. They took their seat and waited to be called.

"Senaj, I know Akuchi told you that I apologized but I want you to hear it from me. I don't know what I was thinking when I put my hands on you and second guessed your loyalty. I'm sorry and I miss you." Reign said with a slight pout.

Senaj looked down at Reign and there was no doubt that he missed her too. He hated that he stayed away for a week. He should have just put it to the side and went over to her house just to make sure that her and the baby were okay. That was a *should'a-would'a-could'a* situation, but he knew now that he wasn't going to let that affect him missing Reign's pregnancy anymore.

"I miss you too and I accept your apology." Senaj simply said and placed a hand on her stomach, immediately causing the baby to move about. At that moment nothing else mattered to the two parents except for what was happening in that current moment.

"Reign?" The nurse called.

Both Senaj and Reign looked up and followed the nurse into the exam room. The nurse weighed her, checked her vitals, asked a few questions and was out of their way.

"We should go get something to eat after this. Oh, wait, do you have to go back to work after this?" Reign asked.

"Nah, I got the rest of the day off. We could go eat. Where do you want to go?"

"Is it bad that I want to go to an all you can eat buffet so that I could just pig out on a bunch of shit?"

With laughter, Senaj said, "No, it's not bad. You get a pass because you're pregnant."

"Oh hush." Reign said joining in with his laughter.

"Knock! Knock! Hello, Reign, it's nice to see you here. And you must be the father." Reign's doctor asked turning to Senaj.

Senaj nodded and shook the doctor's hands.

The doctor started his exam on Reign and made sure that everything was good with mommy and baby. "Okay, I see that everything is good with mommy and baby so we're going to have the ultrasound tech come in here and tell you guys whether you're going to have a boy or a girl. Congratulations, dad." The doctor spoke and shook Senaj's hand again.

"I can't wait." Senaj said, once again rubbing Reign's stomach.

Ten minutes later, the ultrasound tech came inside the room. He set up the machine and had Reign lay on her back. Senaj stood at Reign's side and held her hand as the tech put blue gel on her stomach. She jumped at how cold it was. As the tech moved the wand across her stomach, he explained that he was measuring the baby just to make sure that it was growing at the rate it was supposed to be.

"Okay, are you guys ready to find out what's the sex of the baby is?" The tech asked.

Senaj and Reign looked at each other and in unison said, "Yes."

After a few clicks on the machine, he turned the monitor to them and said, "It's a girl."

Reign stared at the monitor and felt the warmness from her own tears sliding down her face. She was having a little princess as she had always dreamed she would. She looked up at Senaj and saw the smile on his face. For Senaj, he didn't care of the sex of the baby as long as it was healthy. He always wanted a daughter, and this was a bonus for him. The rest of the doctor's visit went by in a breeze and they soon found themselves taking their seats at the buffet.

"Are you ready to stuff your face?" Senaj asked.

"Oh, hell yeah! You don't have any idea how long I've been waiting to do this." Reign squealed with excitement.

Senaj laughed and grabbed Reign by the hand. They piled food onto their plates— crab legs, shrimp, steamed vegetables, fried chicken, chicken and broccoli, and fried rice, just to name a few things. They once again took their seats and began to chow down.

Senaj happened to look at Reign and noticed she was in deep thought. "What's wrong, love?" Senaj asked taking a gulp of his iced tea.

"Nothing much. Just trying to sort something through."

"Like what? Talk to me."

Reign exhaled and went back and forth, debating on if she should tell him what had been on her mind for the past week and a half. She began to open her mouth but a figure standing next to her stopped her. She looked up and noticed a very beautiful female.

Senaj, whose face was deep in his plate, realized Reign hadn't said anything. When he looked up, his heart dropped to his ass.

"Yes, can we help you?" Reign asked politely.

"I'm sorry, he looks like this guy I used to date in college. His name was Senaj and. Oh my God! It is you, Senaj!" Christina exclaimed.

Reign's face tightened as her eyes were directed to Senaj. If looks could kill, Senaj would have dropped dead in that moment.

"Christina," Senaj said, only it came out as if he was seething.

"It's so good to see you. I see that you are on a date though. Why don't you come by my salon, so we could catch up as old friends?" Christina said. When she knew that she had only his attention, she winked at him and placed her card on the table, closer to Reign then Senaj purposely.

After Christina walked away, Senaj looked up at Reign who appeared calm but was brewing with fire on the inside.

"I'm ready to leave." She simply said. She got up and walked out, leaving Senaj behind.

He got up and went to settle the bill before he walked to his car. Reign was standing next to the driver's side biting down on her lip.

"I don't know what—" Senaj began.

Reign interrupted. "I don't care what that was. I can assure that she comes around again, pop up anywhere that we are again, or you show up to that bootleg salon that she got, I promise she's going to be in a world of regret when she meets with my twins. I lost my appetite, but I will not let that bitch ruin one of the happiest days of my life. I'm glad we drove in separate cars. Meet me at my house and we can finish our day with being in bed and watching movies."

Reign eyed Senaj and walked away to her car. She wanted to be mad with Senaj, but she knew he had no control over what Christina did. She made her way to her house thinking about what she could do to Christina. She could practically feel Christina's skin on her hands as she peeled it off her body. Reign threw it deep down in her gut that Christina was for sure going to be a problem. Just how much, Reign wasn't sure of.

Mimi

Chapter Twelve

Pearl sat in the hot police department, waiting to speak with Detective Winslow. She was one week from giving birth to her precious baby boy. This was her last meeting she was having with him and then she was leaving New York. After hearing that James was dead, she knew that she had to go before Reign was after her. Waiting twenty minutes, Detective Winslow finally was able to see her. She followed behind him to his office with her belly leading the way.

"Ms. Marshall, what can I do for you today?" He asked.

She knew she never told him her last name, so she knew that he had did some digging. "Detective Winslow, first I want to say thank you for your time. I was only wondering if you had linked the Lipstick Killah to Reign Mills yet?" Pearl asked being straight forward.

"I can see where your concern is coming from but being that you are not a colleague of mine, I cannot divulge that information to you."

"Well why not? I am helping you with this case. In fact, I have new information for you. But seeing that you can't help me, I can't tell you what I know."

Detective Winslow sat back in his seat and wondered if what Pearl knew was of value. He tapped a pen on his desk and asked, "What do you know?"

"That's not how we are going to play it today, Detective. I want to know—"

"We have not connected her to being the Lipstick Killah yet. We've had some people watching her movements and besides her going to doctor appointments and out to a bunch of different places to eat, she's clean. I'm sorry that you have that in your mind that she's who we want, but she is no longer a person of interest." He said, laying it out for Pearl.

Pearl twiddled her thumbs. "She killed her uncle James. The dude that was found in the abandoned warehouse out in Jersey."

"How do you know this?"

"Believe me, I wasn't there when it happened, but when she found out that her uncle was trying to set her up, she vowed that she would get him before he got her. One night we were hanging out at my house, he came by shooting. For months she placed me in a hotel. She left after she found out that her boyfriend tried to have sex with me. Here is a picture of my window after he had shot it out. Reign had it fixed."

Detective Winslow took all of this in and thanked Pearl. Pearl figured that it was best for her to go. Her plan didn't prove to be as effective as she thought it would be. She gave up. She thanked the detective and walked out of the station. She had parked her car a few blocks away from the station, so she headed in that direction. She felt a queasiness in her stomach, so she rubbed her belly and silently assured her baby that she was on her way to get something to eat. Not paying attention to her surroundings, within seconds from her car, she felt a cloth-like bag, maybe a pillowcase, being placed over her head. She didn't fight, she simply let her kidnapping happen. She knew it was men that was taking her, and she knew it was Reign's order. They were being too gentle with her.

Pearl sat inside a van for what seemed like an eternity. They must have taken every street imaginable that had pot holes, but they made sure that she was uncomfortable. An hour must have lapsed when finally, the van stopped. She heard the two men's muffled conversation outside the van and then the doors opened. Still without a fight, she allowed them to help her out. Not once did she ask any questions. Why would she? She knew exactly what was going on. They walked on top of a rocky pavement and made it inside a building. When they got to their destination, they sat Pearl down on a chair and bound her ankles to the legs and her hands around the back. Once they made sure she was secured, they took the pillowcase off her head. Pearl's first instinct was to look around to see where she was, but the bodies that hung from the ceiling stopped her from doing so. Staring back at her was her mother, brother, and sister. They were already dead from the looks on their faces. Each of their fingers had been cut off, throats were slit, and the ropes tied around their necks were tight. Tears exploded from her eyes. Footsteps walking into the basement-like room caused Pearl to lift her head. There in front of her stood a pregnant Reign.

"Reign, I'm so sorry. I didn't mean for anything to happen. I was only trying to get your attention." Pearl cried.

"So, you went to the fucking pigs?" Reign growled as she landed a right hook to Pearl's jaw. It wasn't hard enough to break it, but it did shatter Pearl's teeth, knocking some loose.

"You wouldn't answer my calls!" Pearl cried.

"And you don't know where I live?"

Damn, why didn't I think about just popping up at her house? That would have made more sense, Pearl thought. She was rendered speechless because she absolutely had no rebuttal at all.

Reign raised her eyebrow, waiting for Pearl to respond. When she didn't, Reign pulled Akuchi to the side and whispered to him.

"Reign, please don't hurt me. I'm going to be giving birth to my baby next week please." Pearl pleaded. All that fell on deaf ears. Pearl watched the bigger guy of the two, wheel out what appeared to be a gurney. Another person walked into the room dressed in scrubs. As what was about to happen registered in Pearl's mind, she began to scream out for help.

"Pearl, there is absolutely no way anyone will be able to hear you. Shut your mouth before this doesn't end well." Reign said. As an afterthought she said, "Well, things aren't going to end well."

Reign nodded to Akuchi and Jamori and they made their way to Pearl. Jamori placed a piece of duct tape over her mouth as Akuchi began to cut the ties on her legs. They carried a squirming Pearl to the gurney and strapped her legs and arms down.

Reign walked close to Pearl and looked down at her in pity. "You know all of this could have been avoided if you would have been women enough to knock on my door. We grew up together. I considered you to be my little sister. How could you do this to me? What was it, Pearl? Jealously? Envy? I always made sure that you were straight. Our kids were supposed to grow up together." Reign stated as tears formed in her eyes. She quickly wiped them away. She continued, "Thanks to you, they will. You just won't be able to witness it."

Reign moved away from Pearl. She could hear her muffled screams as she took her seat in the chair that Pearl previously occupied. Reign watched as the doctor cut into Pearl's stomach, getting ready to deliver Pearl's baby. Pearl's muffled screams tortured Reign the whole twenty minutes it took for the doctor to take the baby out. Reign watched as the doctor scrubbed the baby off, while a nurse came in to wait for the baby. She was riding with Akuchi back to Reign's house where they had transferred her office downstairs into a nursery. There, they were going to weigh and measure the baby, feed him and put him to sleep. Nana and Jackie were going to watch the baby until Reign came home.

"Would you like for me to stich her up?" The doctor asked.

"Nah. We done here." Reign spoke. Reaching into her knee-high boot, she produced a throwing star and it lodged into the doctor's throat. Reign walked over to Pearl and watched as she tried to stay conscious. Reign removed the tape from Pearl's mouth.

"I never thought it would ever come to this." Pearl managed to say.

"You knew the consequences when you first met with that detective. Your fate was written in stone since then. You fuck with me once, shame on me. Fuck with me two times and that's on you, baby girl. My reach is far. Sorry that your family had to suffer at your hands."

A pool of blood began to form in Pearl's mouth. She turned her head to drain it as she spoke, "Just make sure that my baby is well taken care of."

Reign nodded and decided that Pearl wasn't even worth a bullet. She wanted her to bleed out and feel every bit of pain. Before Reign walked away, Pearl raised her hand. Reign knew exactly what Pearl was indicating. For the last time, they shared their handshake that they made up when they were just fourteen years old.

When they were finished, Reign started to walk away until Pearl called her name. Reign turned around and listened to what Pearl had to say. It was the least she could do.

She said, "My son isn't Stanley's. He is James' son."

***

Reign made it home and immediately jumped in the shower. Her whole body was under the flow of the water and she allowed her tears to flow with it. Her thoughts were filled with the day's event. Her ex-best friend's son had her enemy's blood flowing through his veins. That didn't mean she would harm the baby. She wouldn't ever hurt a child. It was just heavy on her heart. That and the fact that this was her first time without leaving her calling card.

Reign scrubbed her body clean and turned the water off. She wrapped a towel around her body and entered her room. Nana must have wheeled in the baby while she was in the shower. She looked down at the precious baby boy as he slept peacefully. Jackie, Jamori, and Nana came inside the room with smiles donning their faces.

"Ugh, what ya'll want? I can't even take a shower in peace." Reign said.

"Oh, shut up. We only came in here to see if you had a name for him." Jamori said.

Reign thought about it. Ever since she found out that she was having a girl, she only thought of a girl's name. Then it clicked in her mind. She said, "Kahlil Bernard Mills."

"After your father?" Nana asked.

"Yes." Reign turned to her cousins and said, "I have something to tell you guys though."

"What's up?" They asked in unison.

"Kahlil is ya'll little brother."

The room grew silent as they all looked at each other. Nana was the first to speak. "Ain't this bout some bullshit!"

"What?" Jackie asked with disbelief.

"Pearl announced it as I was leaving. The baby has nothing to do with anything that their parents had going on. I am still going to take care of Kahlil as if I birthed him myself. It's totally up to ya'll if ya'll want to deal with him." Reign said hoping that they would want to. She wouldn't be having her child until November and she would need them to be her moral support.

"Reign, hell yeah. I want to fuck with this baby. Jackie been stuck to my hip since the womb!" Jamori exclaimed.

Jackie agreed with him and they both raced over to the bassinet like little kids.

Nana's morals were different. As soon as she found out that the baby was by one of her enemies, she would have done away with the child. But, only because her grandchildren were overly excited, she decided to let this one slide. "Now, you need to call your man. Hopefully he is as understanding as these two."

"As soon as ya'll get out, I'm calling him to come over. I know he'll come around."

"Okay." Nana said and made her way to her room.

"Can ya'll get out so I can actually put some clothes on?"

Jackie looked up at Reign and asked, "Can we take him?"

"No. He's sleeping. Let a sleeping baby sleep. When he wakes up, ya' can have him." She watched as Jackie and Jamori walked out of her room. She chuckled as she took her towel off and got into some comfortable house clothes.

Picking up her phone and remote control, she decided to give Senaj a phone call. It rang until the voicemail picked up. She left him a message telling him to call her. Throwing her phone to the side, she laid down and soon fell into a slumber.

Mimi

Chapter Thirteen

Senaj sat with his best friends at their favorite spot. He needed somebody to talk to and fast and without judgement, like he knew his brother would, if he had spoken to him. They had already been hanging at Small's for about an hour just kicking it and catching up. All the while Senaj was trying to figure out where he would begin.

"Senaj, you aiight, man? You look kind of down." Polite questioned.

Rasheed turned his attention to Senaj and noticed the look on his best friend's face. *Here we go with this shit with his psychotic killer girlfriend,* Rasheed thought.

"I'm cool ya'll." He responded.

"No, you're not. Lately it seems like you call us down here when you got something heavy on your mind." Rasheed stated while taking a shot of Patron.

Knowing he was caught he might as well had come clean. "I think I fucked up ya'll." Senaj admitted.

"How so?" Polite asked.

"I went to Christina's salon."

Rasheed almost spat his beer out as both Polite and Rasheed exclaimed, "What?"

"Bro, what you go see that nut for?" Polite asked.

"To be honest, I needed to speak with somebody who doesn't know anything about mine and Reign's relationship. She was there and listened."

"Did you fuck?" Rasheed asked with a smile on his face.

"No, man! It wasn't like that. Like I said, I wanted to speak with someone who wasn't a mutual person. No one to take my side, no one to take hers. And surprisingly, she did just that."

"So how you fucked up?" Polite asked.

"Well, Reign and I found out that we were having a girl. After her doctor's appointment, Reign wanted to go to a Chinese buffet. Being that we have been having so many disagreements about things, I figured that this would be a good way to get everything out in the open and squash it. For the sake of her not being stressful while being pregnant. We just getting our food and Reign was about to tell me all the heavy shit that was on her mind and then she just got quiet on me. I look up and Christina was standing there."

Rasheed and Polite couldn't believe what Senaj was telling them. The Christina that they knew was shy and quiet, so it was new to them to hear about her doing something so boldly. They looked at Senaj intently, waiting for him to finish.

"Did Reign flip? Nigga, you can't just stop there." Rasheed said. He needed to know what happened.

Senaj chuckled lightly and said, "Nah, she didn't flip. Reign just glared at me, and after Christina threw her card down asking me to come to her salon so we could catch up as 'old friends', she said that she was ready to go. She basically said if I go to the salon or if she sees Christina anywhere that we go out, Christina was going to be in a world of regret when she meets Reign's twins. And for the life of me, I don't know if she was talking about her twin cousins or her guns."

Polite said, "Knowing who your girl is, I'm pretty sure that she was talking about her heat. You better be careful, bro, 'cause Reign ain't the type of chick you could just get away with fucking around on."

Senaj exhaled. This was something that he knew already. He shouldn't have gone to that damn salon. Now he was in a fucked-up predicament. Twenty minutes later, Rasheed and Polite were ready to go. Senaj, not so much. The next day he had off and for once he wanted to enjoy himself with a few drinks by himself and get his thoughts together. He slapped fives with his boys as they left. He ordered himself another shot of Patron and listened to the Jazz band that was playing that night.

An hour later, Senaj was toasted. He was so drunk that he could barely stand. As he sat at the bar, he took out his cell phone and went to his text messages. Going to Reign's name he opened it and sent a text message that read: *Sorry it's late beautiful and I know that you need your rest, but I had one too many drinks and I need you to come and get me from Smalls.* Within seconds, Reign responded that she was on her way and for him to sit tight. Senaj knew he would hear it when he woke up in the morning but that was a risk he was willing to take. Senaj didn't know how but one minute he was at the bar, the next he was in the car, and then home.

"I know you're going to be mad at me, but I'll deal with it in the morning. I just want to cuddle with you and rub on your booty." Senaj spoke as he got out of his clothes. He laid on his back on the bed and watched as Reign got out of her clothes. His legs hung over the bed and Reign stood in between them.

"Now you know you want to do more than rub my booty." She said. Reign kneeled between his legs and pulled his flaccid penis out of the top of his boxers. Her small hands wrapped around it and moved up and down in a twisting motion.

Senaj closed his eyes and enjoyed his hand job that he was receiving. His dick swelled in her hand. After moments of him being rock hard, she leaned over him with her ass in the air, she placed his mushroom head in between her lips and gently swirled her tongue around the tip. Senaj raised one hand and placed it in her hair. His penis went further into her mouth and before he knew it, he was down her throat and she was massaging his balls with her free hand.

"Damn, girl, I knew you missed me, but I didn't know that much." He grunted. As her head bobbed, he helped her out just a little bit by palming the back of it. Her mouth felt so good wrapped around his dick that his toes were curled.

Taking his dick out of her mouth, she said, "I'm gonna get back to that. I want to feel you inside of me."

Senaj stood up and bent her over the side of the bed. Grabbing her ass cheeks, he looked down and saw her pretty pussy staring back at him. His mouth practically started to salivate at the sight. He guided himself to her and entered her. In his drunken mind, her pussy was super tight and gripped him like a vice grip. Placing his foot on the bed, he drilled inside of Reign like a jack hammer. Her moans drove him crazy as he forced himself not to cum so fast. Her pussy was excessively wet and tight.

"Harder, Senaj." She moaned.

He did just that as he wrapped his hand around the back of her neck. Her moans turned to screams of pleasure. Soon after, he felt her walls tighten and his dick slipped from her clutches as she squirted all over herself, the bed, and Senaj.

She rolled over onto her back and looked intently at Senaj. "Cum on me." She said as her legs slowly slid open and she used her index and middle finger to bring herself to orgasm again.

Senaj was still a bit fucked up and was seeing double at that point, but he still did what she asked of him. Wrapping his own hand around his own penis, he began to jerk off. Watching her please herself turned him on to the max. He moved closer between her legs and reached down to rub his hands against her mounds. She squealed with pleasure as he pinched her nipples between her fingers. Senaj's hand moved faster as he felt himself about to explode. He squeezed her tittie as he squeezed the head of his penis and landed his seeds all over her stomach and chest. She squirted all over the place again.

"Damn!" Senaj exclaimed and dropped onto the bed. Soon, he was out like a light.

***

Senaj woke up to his phone constantly ringing. He knew he didn't have to be into work that day, so he didn't understand who could be blowing his phone up. He laid there with his eyes closed before he decided on if he wanted to answer or not. Flashes from the previous night with Reign played like a motion picture in his mind causing a smile to spread across his face. The agonizing shrills of his phone caused his eyes to spring open.

"Hello." He said.

"Yo, bro, where are you at?" Akuchi asked into the phone.

"I'm home. What's wrong?" Senaj asked looking for his clothes.

"You home and you ain't just hear me banging on the door? Bro, shit is all bad. Nana got shot last night. Them niggas that was sitting outside your crib that night when Reign hit you, came blasting. Pablo's people coming back for Reign knocking him off in the restaurant."

"What?" Senaj yelled.

"I don't know where you at and what you are doing but you need to get to the hospital ASAP."

"Why are you saying that? I'm home." Senaj said and for the first time he looked around the bedroom. This wasn't his bedroom. *Where the fuck am I?* he thought as his heart proceeded to drop to his feet. He heard Akuchi talking but wasn't listening. He hung up and located his clothing.

As he was putting his socks on, in walked Christina. "Why are you in such a hurry?" She asked, scaring Senaj whose back was turned.

"Ahhh! What the fuck am I doing here? How did I get here?"

"You texted me, asking me to come to pick you up from Smalls. You don't remember?"

"No! I sent that message to Reign; how did you get that?" He asked finally fully dressed.

Christina reached for her phone that was on the nightstand. She opened her text messages and showed Senaj. She said, "No, you sent it to me."

There it was, staring back in his face. His head began to pound as the moment he knew that he fucked up registered.

Christina stood there with a smile on her face.

"Oh no. This isn't good! Did we um—"

"Yes, and it was as amazing as the old times."

"Christina, this was a mistake. I apologize for the whole mix up but if I knew it was you, this wouldn't have happened. I have to go." He grabbed his wallet and keys and flew out of the door. Luckily for him a cab was rounding the corner. He hailed it and got in, heading to Brooklyn Hospital. His phone beeped with a bunch of messages from Christina. He beat himself up about drinking so much and not being aware. Senaj called Rasheed.

"It's kind of early; what do you want?" Rasheed asked into the phone.

"Bro, I need a favor."

"What?"

"Please, if anything happens, I was with you and Polite at Smalls. I got too drunk and went back to your crib since it's closer to the club."

"What did you—ooh, you gonna be in trouble!" Rasheed hollered into the phone.

"Not right now. Just cover for me."

"You know I got you."

"Thank you." Senaj said and hung up the phone.

***

After Reign's brief nap, she felt better. She turned her TV on and they were covering six bodies found in a ditch, burned. She turned the channel because she knew exactly who that was. Climbing out of the bed, she walked over to the bassinet and realized the baby was gone. She rolled her eyes because she knew exactly where he had gone. After brushing her teeth and splashing water on her face, she made her way downstairs. In the living room was everybody, including baby KB and Akuchi.

"Akuchi, shouldn't you be over at your brother's house instead of being here all the time?" Reign asked, pushing his head playfully.

"My brother is always at work or here when ya'll not having ya'll issues." Akuchi stated.

"Stop lying. You know you trying to get in where you fit in with Jackie." Jamori laughed.

"Hey! Please don't do this shit where ya'll talk about me right in front of my face." Jackie said getting up from the couch.

Nana joined in the laughter.

Bok! Ttsh! Bok! Ttsh!

Chaos erupted around them as the front window shattered. Jackie cradled baby Kahlil and ran into the nursery. Nana, Jamori, and Reign ducked behind the couches as they waited for the gunfire to cease. There had been no letting up. Whoever this was came with a vengeance.

"You stupid black bitch! You killed my father!" The person yelled.

That gave them enough time to shoot back. They let them things go through the broken window only to catch the car skidding down the block.

"We need to get everybody out of here! Jackie!" Jamori yelled.

She came from the back with a sleeping baby strapped to her chest. She said, "I already packed Kahlil somethings and formula. Hotel?"

"Yes." Reign said.

"Nana can you—Nana?" Jamori said.

During the chaos, Nana was hit in the chest, close to her heart. Everyone's time slowed down as they rushed to Nana's side. There was a faint pulse. Akuchi jumped in. He was hurt but not as bad as the others were. Chi was just getting to know the sweet old lady, who says whatever comes to her mind.

Akuchi grabbed a crying Jackie by the arms and said, "Listen, Ma, you have to get Kahlil out of here fast. Go get a room and when I get these two straight and your grandmother to the hospital, I'm going to come to the hotel. Just make sure you text me where you at. I need you to be strong and get him out of here, okay, Ma?"

"Okay." Jackie sulked using the back of her hand to wipe the snot and tears from her face. She grabbed the two bags she packed for the baby in under a minute and left.

Akuchi knew that the cops were going to be there soon. He picked up their heat and placed them in a suitcase. He put the suitcase inside the trunk of the car. He went back in the house and saw Jamori doing CPR and Reign was trying to apply pressure to stop the bleeding.

"Listen, we got to go. Ya'll get in the car and I'm gonna be right out." Akuchi stated.

They followed Akuchi's orders and soon after, he came out carrying their grandmother. Jamori put the car in drive and drove like a mad man to the hospital. Reign rarely prayed but as she sat next to Jamori, she couldn't help but to. She had prayed for so long and hard that by the time she opened her eyes, they were at the hospital. Jamori parked the car and they all got out with Akuchi carrying Nana.

"I need some help! She's been shot!" Akuchi yelled once through the emergency sliding doors.

Moments later, nurses and doctors took over by wheeling a gurney over to Akuchi. He placed Nana on the gurney as they watched them intubate Nana to help her breath.

Akuchi turned to Jamori and Reign and said, "Listen, I got heat in the car. I'm going to take care of that and meet up with Jackie. Reign, try to get in touch with Senaj and let him know what is going on. I'll take care of the baby until ya'll find out what's going on with Nana."

Reign reached up and hugged him. She whispered a thank you to Akuchi and pulled away to give Senaj a phone call. This was the second time that he didn't answer his phone, but she couldn't worry about it. Jamori and Reign took a seat and waited. They knew that the police were going to be there soon to question them. It was going to be a long night.

***

Senaj got into the hospital and went straight to the ICU. He instantly felt death in the air as he saw his distraught girlfriend and cousins. They all looked at nothing in particular and sat quietly. Both Reign and Jamori still had on their blooded clothes from the night before. He felt awful that he wasn't there. He was as drunk as a skunk and out, unintentionally cheating on his girlfriend. Slowly he walked over with his hands in his pants pockets. "Is Nana okay?" He asked drawing attention to himself.

They all looked at him, but Reign's eyes were the only one that lingered. "Where were you?" Reign asked. She had bags under her eyes and this was the worse that Senaj had ever seen her and it broke his heart.

"I'm so sorry, babe. The fellas and I went out to Smalls last night. I got way too fucked up and ended up staying with Rasheed last night."

"Explains why you smell like that and why my calls went unanswered."

"Have you eaten?"

"Senaj, my grandmother is laid up in the hospital on a breathing machine. She was shot, and we don't even know if she's going to make it through the day. I am still in the same clothes from yesterday with her blood soaked into them. You tell me. Does it look like I've eaten?" She said while rolling her eyes. At that moment Reign smelled something that turned her stomach and she threw up bile right on the floor.

"If you don't want to eat, get some fluids in you."

"She needs to eat. She's pregnant." Akuchi said walking up to them. He held Kahlil in one arm and held his baby bag on his shoulder. He passed Kahlil to Jackie and grabbed Senaj by his collar and dragged him down the hallway.

"Nigga, if you don't get the hell off me." Senaj said while swatting at his brother's hands.

For the first time that day, Reign, Jackie, and Jamori laughed. Akuchi didn't let Senaj go until they were in the elevator heading to the cafeteria.

"Besides being at work, why are you never around your pregnant girlfriend?" Chi asked.

"Is this why you felt the need to drag me like I'm some fucking kid?"

"Nigga, that's how you are acting. I understand you in your bag because she still doing what she is doing, but come on my nigga, she need you there."

"She told you to say that?"

"Nigga, no. Man, you worried about the wrong thing. She might lose her grandmother; she's an emotional wreck, bro.

Get your priorities together and worry about that small shit later. Make sure she eats, rub her feet, and listen to her, bro. That's all females want."

Senaj understood what his brother was saying. He realized he was slipping before what happened with Christina. Christina was a huge mistake and he knew that. Christina wasn't going to let this go.

"I fucked up bad, bro." Senaj admitted.

"What you mean?" Akuchi asked as they exited the elevator.

"When you asked me where I was, I thought that I was home. I was wasted last night, and I texted Reign. Well, I thought that it was Reign."

Akuchi's mouth hung open and he looked at Senaj with disappointment. He asked, "Bro, please don't tell me that you did what I think you did with who I think you did it with. And then you bring your ass in funky, smelling like you've been living in a liquor warehouse, pussy juice still on your dick. Please tell me you used a condom?"

"Man, I don't know. I was fucked up and thought she was Reign. More than likely I didn't because Reign and I haven't used condoms in months, obviously."

"Reign is going to kill you. And you know what, I might just won't stop her."

"Wait, who's baby were you carrying?"

Akuchi wanted to spill the beans. He simply shook his head and told Senaj that he was keeping his mouth shut. It was funny to Senaj, how he could have so much to say about what was going on in his brother's life, but he couldn't tell Senaj where the hell the baby came from.

Senaj picked up some chicken tenders and fries with an orange juice for Reign, and Akuchi picked up the same thing for the twins. Without another word, they made their way back up to the ICU until they heard screaming and yelling, once off the elevator.

Jackie sat in a chair rocking back and forth as silent tears fell from her eyes. Jamori's back was against the wall as his hands covered his face. Reign was the one that was screaming. She had fallen to her knees as the news of Nana passing hit them all hard. Senaj and Akuchi ran up to them to console them. Although the surgery went well, the doctor's feared that it would take a toll on her heart. It wasn't the bullet that killed her, it was a heart attack. Each of them had a piece of Nana with them.

"Let me find a doctor to find out what's going on." Akuchi said.

"It was a heart attack." Jackie sobbed.

"Everything is going to be okay. Did ya'll go and see her?" Senaj asked.

"No. They said they would give us time. There isn't enough time for us to be prepared to see her like that. The only person that was as close as to my father that I could get." Reign expressed. Her heart was aching and Senaj felt like a dick head.

He kneeled next to Reign and held her. Her body shook in his arms and his heart cried out for her. Heavy footsteps coming in their direction captured Senaj's attention and he turned around. Cops were coming fast in their direction.

"Are you all the family of Joanna Mills?" They asked.

Jamori wiped his face and stood up. "Yes, we are. What can we do for you?" He asked.

The officer extended his hand for Jamori to shake but Jamori just looked at it as if his hand was crawling with some flesh-eating bacteria.

Drawing his hand back, the officer said, "We just had a few questions for you all."

Senaj stood up with his hands in his pockets. He said, "With all due respect, officer, they just lost their grandmother who, might I add, they were all close to. I'm pretty sure that they cannot help you at this present moment. Please leave them a card and I will make sure that they will contact you."

The officer looked on at Senaj with distaste, because in his head, who did this black monkey think he was talking to? While he tried to be a good cop, Officer Paul Burke was an undercover racist. His face flushed red and even though Senaj simply asked that the police let his family grieve, Paul Burke thought Senaj was acting pompous and more of an authority figure than he was. Paul Burke lost himself in a vision of himself squeezing the life out of Senaj. His partner speaking brought him back to reality.

"We understand that this is a hard time for all of you. This is a homicide case being that your grandmother has now passed on. You have my, our, condolences. Please give us a call so that we could ask you guys a few questions. Here is my card." The second officer— officer Bryson Dillard— saw where this was heading so he knew he had to act fast if he didn't want his partner to fly off the handle.

Senaj reached for the card that the officer was handing to him.

"You do know that you are talking to the officers of the law, right?" That was Paul.

"Yes, sir. I know exactly who I am talking to. If you are insinuating that I was being disrespectful, that wasn't the case." Senaj responded.

Reign stood up from the floor and was now standing along with Jackie, Jamori, and Akuchi.

"Paul, let it go." Bryson mumbled.

"No, Bryson. These young nig-fellas need to learn how to respect the law."

"With all respect, sir, I didn't say anything that was offensive." Senaj said. His heart pounded in his chest because he felt it in his bones that something was going to go horribly wrong.

"You thugs and punks think that you all run these streets!" Senaj couldn't believe what was going on and to defuse the situation, he decided to just stay quiet and walk away. Placing his hand in his pocket to grab his wallet to put the cop's card inside but was frozen in fear when officer Dillard pulled his gun and started yelling.

"Get your hands out of your pockets right now! Hands in the air!" He yelled.

"Sir, I am reaching for my wallet. I am just going to place your partner's card in there." Senaj said. Surprisingly, his voice was calm.

"This is getting out of hand, Paul. Stand down!" Bryson yelled. His hand was on his gun but not out of his holster.

"Nigger, take your hand from your pockets!"

Reign asked, "What did you just say?"

"Babe, please stand back." Senaj looked at Bryson and continued, "I'm taking my hands from my pockets. I will not have anything in my hands."

Bryson felt for Senaj. Bryson was one of the good cops. He nodded but he didn't make sure that his partner understood to stand down.

Senaj slowly took his hands form his pocket and as soon as his hands were chest high— *pop, pop, pop.*

Bryson looked at his partner and shook his head, running to Senaj's side. The hospital erupted in chaos. Reign lunged at Paul but Akuchi stopped her. Before Paul knew what was going on, doctors rushed to Senaj's side, checking him to make sure that he was okay. Bryson called it in and he knew once his captain showed up, not only would Paul be in hot water, he knew he would be too.

The doctors cut Senaj pants leg where he was shot to evaluate the damage and then placed him on the gurney and rolled him away. Reign stared at Dillard, committing his face to her memory. She was making sure that she would get at him later. Ten minutes after Senaj was shot, the police swarmed the hospital. Reign, Akuchi and the twins watched on as the captain pulled the two officers to the side to question them. Jackie walked over and politely interrupted their conversation. Everyone else looked on and wondered what Jackie was doing. Not too long after, Jackie walked back with the captain.

"I am tremendously sorry about what happened here today. Please inform me of what happened here so that I could deal with this accordingly." Captain said.

Reign folded her arms and said, "Deal with this accordingly? Don't you mean give that prick of an officer of yours a slap on the wrist, give him paid leave, and then let him come back to work? In case you didn't know, Captain, you have a racist pig on your force. We will deal with this accordingly and my lawyer will be in touch." Reign eyed the captain one more time before she walked away to go find out how Senaj was.

The captain smirked that awkwardly and then turned his back.

"That girl is going to kill herself some cops." Jamori stated.

Akuchi and Jackie shook their heads as they slowly followed behind Reign. As soon as things start to look up, there was always something that happens to deter life.

Mimi

Chapter Fourteen

Eight hours after Reign found out about her grandmother passing and her boyfriend being shot by the cops, she was finally able to go home, shower, and feed herself and her child. The amount of stress that she had on her, she knew that her baby could be in harm's way. Reign vowed that she had shed the last of her tears when she was at the hospital.

After she ate, she sat on her couch and watched her curtains flap around due to the air that was blowing. A storm was brewing, and Reign had vengeance on her mind. She took out her cell phone and dialed Jameson's number. The phone rang to voicemail. She hung up and sent him a text with 911 to let him know that it was an emergency. Next up, she called her people to come fix her window. They would be there later that day to do so. She sent Senaj a message asking how he was doing.

Baby Daddy: I'm good but I would be better if you were here.

Me: I'm sorry that I didn't stay. I just needed to get out of there. There was too much that was going on. Did the bullet go through your leg?

Baby Daddy: No. It grazed me, but it was deep. I'll be coming home tomorrow, and they want me to stay off it for a few days.

Me: I could be your nurse. LOL!

Reign's phone rang, interrupting her brief conversation with Senaj. It was Jameson calling back.

"Reign, what's going on?" Jameson asked.

"I need a few things from you. Unfortunately, I need you to meet me at my house."

"Okay. Text me your address and I'll be there as soon as I wrap some things up."

"Okay. Just call when you're out front. I'm gonna attempt to nap."

Jameson said okay while Reign decided to get comfortable on the couch to make it a little easier to fall asleep.

***

The constant beating of the rain on her windows reminded her of what happened that morning when Senaj left her place. The sound of the rain represented how her heart beat in her chest as the one guy that she has ever loved, walked out of her life again. There was a point where she had forgotten all about him, but she couldn't help that her old feelings came flooding back when she saw him at the doctor's office.

When Christina had gotten the text message from Senaj, she had shipped her son to his grandmother's house. He was due back the next day, but the way she felt like she was about to go insane, she would tell her mother to keep him for a tad bit longer. That was until she figured out how she would get Senaj to speak to her. She had been texting him and calling him only to get met with a message that he had blocked her.

It was close to midnight and she had grown restless. Christina had showered and climbed into bed, deciding to watch some TV, which she hadn't done in a while. The first thing that popped up was a shooting at a hospital. Not wanting to watch anything sad, she got ready to turn the channel, until she saw Senaj's face plastered onto the screen. Her hear rate sped up as she listened to the reporters explain what happened. Once they were done, she called the hospital to find out visiting hours and then asked to be transferred to his room. The phone rang four times before he answered.

"Hello."

"Before you decide to hang up, please just give me a few minutes." Christina spat out.

"Who is this? Christina?" Senaj asked through his teeth.

"It is. I saw what happened to you on the news. I was calling to see how you were doing."

"Placing you on block should have given you the indication that I didn't want to speak with you. Christina what happened was a mistake, and I need for you to get that through your head. I don't want to be that guy to you because you don't deserve that, but—"

"So then don't be that guy, Senaj. Leave your girl and be with me. Let's pick up where we left off." Christina interrupted.

"Christina, do you hear yourself? This cannot and will not happen. Please refrain from contacting me. If you do so, you will leave me no choice but to get a restraining order on you."

"You don't want to do that, Senaj." Christina said as she chuckled to herself.

"That's what I'm trying to tell you. But you're pushing my hand."

"No. When I say you don't want to do that, I mean that if you do, you would have to explain to your baby mother why. You would have to explain that you drunkenly texted your ex and had amazing, unprotected sex with her. If that's what you want, then by all means. If not, you would come to your senses and drop that hoe and come on home."

There was a pause before Senaj let out a loud, deep laugh like it came from the pit of his stomach. The smile that was on Christina's face dropped. Senaj said, "That was cute. Nice try though." With that, he hung up the phone which only infuriated Christina.

Senaj was gonna pay for how he just played her to the left like he did. Who did he think he was? After she held the phone to her face for what seemed like hours, she placed it on the charger and thought about ways to get him to see where she was coming from. She thought about it so hard that she even saw it in her dreams.

***

Reign made sure that she got up bright and early to make her way to the hospital to pick Senaj up. The rest of her family stayed home to take care of baby KB and to make plans for Nana's funeral. Reign walked inside of the hospital like she owned it. She was dressed in white linen pants, open-toe Guess sandals, a red blouse, and her hair was in two cornrows, which had become her signature hairstyle. Her wrists dripped with expensive 24k gold bangles as she wore simple square diamond studs in her ears.

"Ma'am, who are you here to see?" The nurse asked Reign when she walked up to the nurse's station.

"Senaj Ademyemi. The one that was shot by the cops last night."

"Yes, ma'am. Here you go." The nurse said and passed Reign a visitor's pass.

Reign grabbed the pass and made her way to Senaj's room. When she got there, he was sitting on the edge of the bed with the same clothes that he had on for two days in a row.

"You need to throw everything you have on in the garbage. I got you a change of clothes. Get up, shower, and get dressed." Reign said causing Senaj to jump.

"Hello and good morning to you too, honey." Senaj said sarcastically, reaching for Reign so he could kiss her.

She smiled brightly as she stood in front of Senaj and between his legs. She placed her lips on his but pulled away with a frown. "I hope they gave you a disposable toothbrush and toothpaste because your breath is on a whole new level." Reign stated while plugging her nose.

Senaj sucked his teeth as he grabbed the bag with his clothes in it, going to the shower. Reign took a seat on the chair near the hospital bed. She took out her cell phone and sent a text to Jameson, asking if he had the information that she needed. He replied within minutes and told her that he did and would meet her in a few hours. There was a knock on the door that caused Reign to advert her attention from her phone.

"Where is Dr. Ademyemi?" The discharge asked.

"Oh, he's just taking a much-needed shower. You could leave the discharge papers and I'll have him sign them. I could bring them up to the nurse's station."

"There is no need for you to go through all of that. I could just come back in ten minutes to pick them up. That's good enough time?"

Reign smiled and said, "Sure. That should be enough time."

The nurse left the clipboard on the rolling table and walked out.

Five minutes later, Senaj emerged from the bathroom smelling better. He wore a pair of blue jean shorts, a white crisp T-shirt, and some all-black Jordan's. Reign passed him some lotion and he cautiously sat on the bed to put it on.

"When we get back to the house, we are going to have to talk about somethings." Reign said while rubbing the back of Senaj's head.

His heart stopped beating and his mouth went dry. "About what, Love?" He asked as calmly as he could as to not make her feel there was anything wrong on his part.

"Just a few things. I don't want to mention them in this room right now." Reign gave him a look that told him exactly what he wanted to know without having to ask another question.

He nodded and picked up his discharge papers. Once he signed them, the nurse came in. She explained to both of them how they were to take care of his wound. He was due back in a week and a half to get his stitches removed. With his prescription for pain pills in his hand, he and Reign left to go home.

By the time they got home, everybody was awake and sitting at the table eating breakfast. Jamori and Akuchi gave Senaj a pound while Jackie gave him a hug. Baby KB was sleeping peacefully in his swing, causing Senaj to ask who baby it was.

"Senaj, I think you should sit down while I explain it to you." Reign said as she stood next to the counter with a bottle of water.

"Umm, okay." Senaj said and took a seat at the table.

"Okay, so you know how Nana had said that there was someone who was talking to the police? That they were dropping hints saying that I was the Lipstick Killah?"

"Yes, I know. You snuffed me because you thought it was me." Senaj said while rubbing his face as if the hit was still fresh.

Reign eyed him and decided to continue. She said, "Yes, but there is no need for you to bring up old shit. Anyway, Nana and I had a talk and she knew who it was that had loose lips and she told me basically that it was Pearl. So, me being me, I went to handle that. The baby had nothing to do with anything. Besides his mother's betrayal, I decided to keep him as my own. After all, he's James' son and I figured that if I kept him, Jackie and Jamori would want to be a part of his life."

Senaj's mouth hung open as he was rendered speechless. He looked down at baby KB and back at Reign. Finally, he was able to form some words together. He said, "Reign, are you crazy? If there was a cop involved and he knew that Pearl was pregnant, when her body turned up, you don't think that you are the first person that he is going to come and question?"

"No, because tonight I'm going to handle him." Reign responded as if she was going to ask this cop for a date.

"That's a cop you are talking about."

"So?"

"So? What do you mean so? This is why I don't want you doing this shit because it seems like all of your common sense goes out of the window."

"Senaj, there is a problem, and this is the only way that I solve problems."

Senaj rubbed his forehead and said, "You know what? You gonna do what you want to do anyway, so it doesn't matter what I say. I need to lay down, I'm starting to get a headache."

"So, go lay down, but tonight whether you like it or not, I'm taking care of this."

"I guess." Senaj said and left the kitchen.

Jackie and Jamori just stared at each either in silence until Reign changed the subject and began to tell them her plan. She needed all of them in on this plan, and whether Senaj liked it or not he was babysitting. By him doing so, he wouldn't know just how much of a bond he would gain with baby KB.

A week later

The church was filled with more than a hundred people, due to Jackie and Jamori who called all of Nana's friends to attend the service. Reign made sure to send her grandmother home in style like she would have wanted. Nana wasn't an ordinary grandmother, so instead of one of those puffy old lady grandma dresses, Reign put her in a spaghetti strapped Fendi monogrammed dress. There was a split in the back and it stopped just below her knees. On her feet were plat-formed, monogrammed matching Fendi peep-toe shoes. Nana's makeup was beat for the gawds and made a few women jealous that her makeup looked so damn good. Nana was laid to rest in a 24k gold casket with chrome accents.

After her body was viewed, her casket was closed, and the pastor began the service. Everyone in the church didn't have a dry eye as they each thought back on the memories that they had with Nana. After the service, it was to the graveyard they went. Only the immediate family were allowed there which was only Reign, the twins, Akuchi, and Senaj. They were paying their own respects without all the extra people. Upon arriving, Reign had six dozen long stemmed red roses sitting around Nana's grave.

"You know, I never saw this day coming. I thought she would out live all of us." Jamori stated with tears forming in his eyes.

"We all believed that, Jamori. But God needed her up there more than we needed her down here. Probably to watch over all of our crazy asses." Jackie declared with laughter.

"Because we don't have not one lick of sense." Reign jumped in. Everything went back to silence as they watched the groundskeeper lower Nana into the ground for her eternal resting space. When she was completely down, they took turns throwing dirt over her casket. Unbeknownst to them, they were being watched closely.

Chapter Fifteen
Three Months Later

Baby KB's wails woke Senaj from his sound sleep. He looked at the time and noticed that it was going on three in the morning. He had to get up in two hours to get ready for work. Reign stirred in her sleep before she sat up. Senaj looked at her and knew that she needed her rest. She was the one who put him to sleep, so it only made sense for Senaj to get up and get the baby. He rubbed Reign's stomach and felt his daughter kick as he assured Reign that he would get Kahlil and for her to get some sleep.

Reign had given her house to the twins and moved in with Senaj because it was the right thing to do. They had a growing family, and, in her mind, the right thing was to move in with Senaj.

Before Senaj went to get Kahlil, he took a bottle out of their mini fridge and put it in the bottle warmer. He rushed inside of the Kahlil's room and picked him up from his crib and placed him against his chest. Instantly Kahlil calmed down his crying and rubbed his face against Senaj's body.

"I know, little man. You hungry, and guess what? Daddy got you a bottle warming up." Senaj grabbed Kahlil's diapers and wipes and made his way back to his room. He looked at Reign briefly and smiled as he saw her sleeping peacefully. Grabbing Kahlil's bottle from the bottle warmer, he made sure that it was the right temperature before he sat down and began to feed him.

Every day it amazed Senaj how fast Kahlil was sucking down his bottle and he knew as he got older, Kahlil was going to eat them out of house and home. Senaj managed to feed him, burp him, change him, and put him back to sleep all under forty-five minutes. Senaj placed him back inside of his crib and climbed back into bed with Reign to get some sleep. He placed his hand on her stomach as he always did when they spooned. A smile was plastered on his face as he felt his princess kicking at his hand. For this, he was grateful.

***

Five o'clock came quicker than what Senaj wanted to. His eyes were heavy and all he wanted to do was lay back down and close his eyes. And he almost did too but something wet on the bed touching his foot kept him up. Turning the lamp on, on his side of the bed and moved the covers, the color from his face drained and his body went numb. For a few seconds, he was stuck until it clicked in his head to check Reign's pulse. It was faint but was still there. The amount of blood that was on the bed was a clear indication that there was something wrong. Before dialing 911, he tried to wake Reign up, but it was a lost cause.

"Nine-one-one, what's your emergency?" The operator said.

"I need an ambulance at 12 Eldert Lane. My girlfriend has a weak pulse, she's unconscious, and she is pregnant. There is blood everywhere!" Senaj yelled, panicking.

"Sir, I need you to calm down."

"Fuck calming down! Send a fucking ambulance right the fuck now!" Senaj yelled into the phone and then hung up. He ran into KB's room and started to dress him as he dialed Akuchi.

"This better be an emergency for you to be calling me at five in the damn morning." Akuchi said when he answered. He looked over at Jackie who was still soundly sleeping.

"It is. I need ya'll to meet me at Jamaica Hospital! Chi, there is blood everywhere!"

Akuchi sat straight up and said, "Bro, we are getting up now. What happened?"

Senaj, not being able to hold his tears back any longer, said, "I don't know what happened. There's blood all over the bed. The ambulance is on its way, meet me there."

Senaj disconnected the phone call and finished getting baby KB dressed. He ran to his apartment door and flew down the hallway to prop the building door open for the fire department and ran back inside his apartment. He packed what he could for Kahlil and placed him in the car seat.

"You called for an ambulance?" The EMT asked while sticking his head through the door.

"Yes. My girlfriend, she's in the bedroom. She's pregnant, has a faint pulse, and she is unconscious." Senaj managed to spit out.

The EMT's flew into the bedroom and began to prep her for an IV.

"What's your girlfriend's name?" A fireman asked.

"Reign Mills, no known allergies to medicine, thirty-two weeks pregnant. I want her to go to Jamaica Hospital. She is twenty-eight years old." Senaj continued to rattle off Reign's information down to him until they brought Reign out of the room on a gurney.

Her beautiful chocolate skin now looked ashy and deprived of color. They had an IV hooked up to her arm and was giving her oxygen.

"Sir, you know you can't bring the baby on the back of the ambulance." An EMT stated once he noticed that Senaj was following close behind them.

"No shit, bitch! I'm following behind ya'll!" Senaj yelled and took off for his car.

The EMTs put Reign inside of the ambulance and made a mad dash for the hospital. Senaj followed close behind the ambulance that when they blew a red light so did he. They arrived at the hospital within ten minutes and rushed Reign into the operating room. Senaj rushed in right after, with Kahlil in his arms.

"Where is she?" He yelled looking around for a familiar face. Finally, he saw one of the EMTs and rushed over to him. "Where is she? What happened? Are they going to be okay?" Senaj asked, firing question after question.

"Sir, calm down. It looks like her placenta erupted and both her and the baby are losing a lot of blood and oxygen. They took her in for an emergency C-section. A doctor will be with you soon for an update. Just try to remain calm and have a seat." The EMT said. He felt bad for Senaj being that he had went through the same thing less than a year ago. He watched as Senaj ran his hand down his face and took a seat on a vacant chair. Grabbing his clipboard, the EMT left the hospital.

Senaj looked down at Kahlil and wondered how he had slept through all the chaos. The tears again cascaded down his face as Senaj became full of fear. He couldn't lose Reign nor his baby girl.

"Senaj!" Akuchi yelled, causing Senaj to look up from Kahlil. Akuchi's heart broke as he saw how distraught his brother was.

Jackie and Jamori followed behind Akuchi.

"Bro. I-I-I can't lose them." Senaj stuttered. The tears wouldn't stop falling.

Jackie swooped in and grabbed Kahlil from Senaj. "We're just going to take a little walk while you two talk. We'll be back." Jackie said. She placed a kiss on Senaj forehead while Jamori patted him on the back.

"Senaj, I know this is hard, but you are not going to lose either one of them. What happened?" Akuchi said.

"The EMT that brought her here said that it looked like her placenta erupted. She lost a lot of blood which put her and the baby at risk. They were both losing oxygen and I don't know if they will be okay. No one has come out to give me an update yet." Senaj said and placed his head in his hands.

"So why don't we ask? Dry your eyes, bro. They will have a great update and you gonna kick yourself in your ass for worrying yourself so much."

"You think so?"

"Of course. You know through whatever happens, everything will be okay and I'm going to be here for you. You want me to call mom and dad?"

"Yes, I'll go and see what's going on."

"Sounds like a plan."

Senaj got up and made his way to the nurse's station and Akuchi called their parents. His mind was a mess as he tried to figure out what he could do to keep Senaj from being a complete mess. His thoughts were deterred when he spoke to his parents. They told Akuchi that they were going to take the first flight that they could catch and would be there soon. As he was hanging up, Senaj was walking back with a solemn look on his face.

"They said that the baby was delivered and is being attached to a breathing machine so that they could give her oxygen and help her breathe. She lost so much oxygen in such a little bit of time. They say they don't know if she's going to make it. They also said that if she does, there is a possibility that she will have growth issues, become brain dead or may even have cerebral palsy." The words were hard to get out since his throat dried up upon hearing the news.

"Reign?" Akuchi asked.

Senaj's eyes misted over and said, "While she was giving birth to Zariyah, she flat lined.

Mimi

Chapter Sixteen

They say when you are dead, you see a bright light. To not go to that bright light because if you do, there is no way you could come back. There was no white light for Reign.

Reign opened her eyes, and everything was bright. Her eyes wandered as she tried to figure out where she was. She sat up on her elbows and noticed that she was laying on grass, and as far as she could see there wasn't anything else around her. Standing up, she wondered where Senaj was and why the hell was she in just a field of nothing but grass.

"Wipe that look off of your face." A familiar voice said from behind her. She turned around and saw her grandmother in the prettiest white dress. Her smile was even brighter, but Reign wore a look of confusion on her face.

"Nana, how am I seeing you right now?"

"How do you think, child?"

Reign wanted nothing in that moment but to pass out. She couldn't be what she thought she was. She was pregnant. She reached for her stomach and didn't feel her bump. Tears sprang to her eyes as she realized what was going on. Her grandmother walked up to her and wrapped her arms around Reign.

"Nana, I don't understand. I was just sleeping with Senaj and baby Kahlil." Reign spoke.

"I know, baby. Your placenta erupted. They delivered the baby—"

"Zariyah lived?"

"Yes, she did. That's a beautiful name."

"I guess I could accept me being gone because I know Senaj is going to take care of Zariyah the best way he can."

"Yes, he will, baby. Come with me." Nana said with the brightest smile on her face. She reached for Reign's hands as the tears began to pour harder down her face.

There was a bright light that appeared in front of them. They began to walk together.

"I wouldn't do that." A deep voice said.

Reign and her grandmother paused in their footsteps. Fear ran through Reign as she debated with herself if she was going to turn around. She thought if she did then she would be face to face with the devil himself. She wouldn't be surprised with all the dirt she has done.

Nana stomped her foot and said, "Dammit, KB."

Reigns eyes widened, and she turned around. There he stood, looking the same that he did when he passed. He looked like he had a fresh cut and he was wearing the crispiest white suit.

"Daddy?" Reign questioned. She couldn't be this lucky to see him again.

"It's me, baby girl." He said with his arms out stretched. Reign ran into his arms and sobbed heavily. She missed him terribly.

"KB, you just can't let me have no fun." Nana huffed and puffed.

"Mama, it ain't about you having fun. It's about being honest."

Reign looked up at her father with wonderment. She asked, "What you mean?"

He chuckled and said, "You didn't die. I mean, you did flat line but right now you're in a medically induced coma."

"A coma?"

"Yes, there was a lot of blood loss. You're going to be fine. Mama, you're a trip."

Nana side-eyed KB and said, "Sorry for scaring you, Reign. But you know Granny couldn't help herself."

"Ugh, you play too much." Reign said with a roll of her eyes.

"Just 'cause your father is standing right there don't mean I won't go upside your head."

"Okay, Mama. She gotta go back now. Her baby and her man are waiting for her. Baby girl, I am proud of who you've become. I'm glad you stuck with what I taught you. You have a couple more people you need to handle; Pablo's son included. There's more enemies heading your way, but I don't doubt that you will handle them. Be careful and I love you oh so much."

The tears dripped down her face again and she couldn't help but to hate herself for it. She had never cried this much ever in her life. As she whimpered, she said, "I love you too, Daddy. You too, Nana. I'm gonna miss you both."

***

It had been three weeks after Reign had given birth to Zariyah. She finally had come out of her coma and she was responding well. Senaj rushed down to the hospital as soon as he had gotten the call that she was awake. Senaj had took a leave from work so that he could take care of Zariyah and Kahlil. The stress of him having to take care of the kids and having to go back and forth to court for the cop that shot him, was taking a toll on him. He was more than happy to hear Reign was okay and well. When Senaj had gotten to Reign's room, he exhaled before he opened the door. He grabbed the door knob and almost went into cardiac arrest once the door was open and he saw what was in front of him.

Announcing his presence, he said, "Christina? What the fuck are you doing here?"

Mimi

The End
Sneak Peek of Lipstick Killah 3: The Finale

Mimi

Chapter One

Dim lights, sterile air, beeping machines, and death lingering in the air. Hospitals had become the norm for Reign and Senaj. Each time the visit would be more complicated than before. While Senaj was grateful that he had his baby girl, the love of his life was in danger. The amount of pain that filled Senaj's chest was unimaginable. Almost losing his child and his future wife in the same day would have sent him into the cuckoo's nest.

"What do you mean she flat lined?" Akuchi asked.

"For five minutes, she was dead. They got her back but now they placed her in a medically induced coma, sust so that she could heal better without any extra stresses." Senaj said.

"Bro, you know she's gonna be fine." Akuchi stated. Even though he wasn't sure of that to be true, he had to believe it just enough to make sure his brother believed it, too.

Jackie walked up to Senaj and gave him a hug, causing Senaj to bury his head into her neck and silently cry. Jackie tried to get it together but as she felt his body shake in her arms, she couldn't hold hers in any longer. Senaj wasn't the only one who was afraid of losing Reign. Although the cousins were just getting to know each other, they had grown to love each other and create a bond that was inseparable.

"When can you see Zariyah?" Jackie asked when she pulled away from Senaj.

They wiped their eyes and sat down next to Akuchi and Jamori, who was holding baby KB.

"I'm a horrible father already. I didn't even think about asking the doctor that. Only thing that was stuck in my mind was the fact that I could have lost Reign." Senaj sobbed.

"Cut that shit out right now. There is just too much going on. All you got to do is ask a doctor." Jackie said.

"Yeah, you're right."

Senaj got up and walked to the nurse's station. He asked to speak with a doctor. A few minutes passed, and a doctor came up to him. Luckily for him, the doctor was able to take him to see his baby girl. His heart boomed against his chest with each step that he took towards the NICU.

"We have managed to stabilize your daughter's breathing machine, but the good thing is that she is showing brain activity. Our plan is to wean her off oxygen for longer periods of time. Of course, we want her to not need it at all. She has a feeding tube for the moment. As we slowly take her off the oxygen, we will try to get her to latch onto a bottle."

"Okay." Senaj simply replied as he tried to keep track of everything the doctor was saying.

Before he was allowed inside of the NICU, the doctor told Senaj to put on a surgical gown, shoe protectors, and a mask. With each passing step, he looked down at each baby in their incubators.

"Here is your baby girl. Right now, you can't hold her but soon she will be able to come out of the incubator for skin to skin contact." The doctor said.

Senaj was in awe and couldn't help to be proud. He said a silent prayer for Reign and Zariyah for a speedy recovery. He needed both home and sooner rather than later. He apologized to Reign under his breath, hoping that she would understand that he would be spending the night with Zariyah.

Two weeks later...

Senaj was finally going to trial for the cop who shot him. It was all over the news and the department even offered him a settlement. He turned it down due to his lawyer telling him not to take it, that he could get him way more than the fifty thousand that they were trying to offer. For Senaj, it wasn't about the money. It was about bringing awareness to racism with cops shooting unarmed black men. It was becoming normal and it wasn't sitting well with him and many black people across America. All he wanted was justice.

By his side were his parents, his brother, and the twins. He sat at the desk with his attorney as they listened to the racist cop's attorney say how Burke felt his life was in danger. This infuriated Senaj to the point where he almost lost his cool. His attorney told him to sit tight and the fact that the jury was sixty percent black, was in his favor. Although everything appeared to be going in his favor, he knew that there was a possibility that something could go wrong. The black people that was on the jury could be Uncle Tom's and his whole case and the justice that he was trying to get would be pointless.

"Court is adjourned until tomorrow." The judge banged his gavel, and everyone stood from their seats.

Senaj felt his father's hand on his shoulder, silently letting Senaj know that everything would be okay.

"I have good news." Senaj's attorney whispered as they spilled into the hallway of the court building.

"What's that?"

"Burke's partner, Dillard, the one that was on the scene, is going to testify tomorrow. I had an inside source tell me that they overheard the captain threaten to fire Dillard if he did testify. I have this in a written statement that even Dillard doesn't know. It will protect him just in case. You know, like a thank you because you didn't have to type of thing. My source told me that he has quit since the captain threatened him and is looking into going to a less racist district."

"Okay, good. If anything changes, please give me a call. My daughter is coming home from the hospital and I have to finish getting things ready for her arrival." Senaj said while shaking his lawyer's hand.

As always, they parted their ways and went in separate directions. The lawyer went out the way where there were reporters, while Senaj and his family went through the exit that didn't have any.

The ride back to Senaj's place was a quiet one. Each with their own thoughts. Senaj's thoughts were always on Zariyah and Reign. All his praying had worked and one of his ladies were coming home. No dependency on oxygen but they were sending Zariyah home with some. They were going to keep a close eye on her in her first year of living and gradually pull back as they saw her progression. Now Senaj just had to work on getting Reign home.

They entered Senaj's apartment one by one, each exhausted from the day's events. Senaj went right into the room that Kahlil and Zariyah would be sharing and took a seat in the rocking chair. He closed his eyes as he wanted to enjoy that moment of peace and quiet.

"Senaj?" A soft voice called from the doorway. He knew who it was automatically. Only the sound of his mother's voice could calm the thundering in his chest besides Reign.

"Yes, Mama?" Senaj asked opening his eyes.

"Can we talk?" She asked.

"Of course." Senaj replied. He got up from the rocking chair and let his mother have his seat. He sat at her feet and put his head on her lap like he used to do when he was a little boy.

"Your father and I were talking and we both agreed that when Zariyah is cleared to travel, the both of you should come stay with us."

That was something that Senaj wasn't expecting. He thought that she was going to give him a few words to at least make him feel better in his situation.

"What?" He questioned, removing his head from her lap.

His mother's face was filled with desperation as she said, "It wouldn't be for long. Until you find a job and your own place."

"Mama, let me get this straight. You want me to take my daughter and move her miles away from her mother, who, might I add, died for five minutes while bringing her into this world, and is still in a coma, healing from delivering her. You want me to leave my son—"

"He is not your son!"

"I adopted him, mom, so you know what that makes us? Father and son! Whether you like it or not. How would you like it if my father, your husband, would have taken Akuchi and I, and left you after you had given birth to us?" Senaj asked. He was enraged, and he didn't want to sound like he was being disrespectful because that was the furthest thing that he wanted his mother to think. But she was pushing his limits.

Zain jumped up from her seat on the rocking chair. She spat, "Regarde ton ton!"

By this time the others had gathered at the room door. Senaj said, "Mama, I'm a grown man. I refuse to watch my tone, especially when you are asking me to leave my family."

"You call her your family but look at everything that has gone on with you since you've met her. You should have just stayed with Christina!" His mother yelled.

Jackie turned to Akuchi and whispered, "Who the fuck is Christina?"

Akuchi eyed her and said, "Nobody."

"I should have stayed with Christina? Funny thing is, mom, she turned to drugs, robbed me, and broke my heart beyond measures imaginable. No thank you!" Senaj yelled.

"That's it! It's final! You will be moving as soon as my granddaughter is cleared to travel!"

"Like hell! She may be your granddaughter but she's my child! Straight from my ball sack!"

"Assez!" Akachi's voice boomed. He had heard and saw enough."

"Oh shit." Jackie whispered.

Akuchi had heard enough. He knew that once his father jumped in, whatever he said was final, despite what or how anyone felt. He turned around and walked away, and even though the nosey in them wanted to stay and listen, Jackie and Jamori followed Akuchi and had no choice to hear form Senaj what happened later.

***

Senaj was just leaving court when he had gotten the call from Reign's doctor, letting him know that she had woken up. He had planned on going home to spend time with Zariyah and Kahlil. It was October, and soon the weather would start to change, and he wanted them to get as much fresh air as they could stand. He called Jackie and asked if she could keep the kids a little while longer as he ran a quick errand. He didn't want to let anyone know the news yet until he laid eyes on her himself.

As he drove to Jamaica Hospital, he thought about his day in court. The jury unanimously came to the decision that Officer Burke was guilty and he would be spending ten to fifteen years in prison. The court room erupted in pandemonium and that's when, for the first time, Senaj knew how much support he had. Not only that, but his family would be suing the police department.

Senaj arrived at the hospital and raced through to find out where she was. A nurse told him that she was moved to a recovery room and gave him the directions. As he made it to her room, his heart pounded in his chest because of the anticipation of seeing Reign awake for the first time in three weeks.

His palms were sweaty, and he was pretty sure that there was sweat forming under his underarms. He opened the door and almost went into cardiac arrest at what was in front of him.

Announcing his presence, he said, "Christina? What the fuck are you doing here?"

Mimi

Chapter Two

"**S**enaj, didn't I tell you what would happen if this woman was to come around me?" Reign asked. She was speaking to Senaj, but she was staring a hole through Christina.

"Yeah, you did." Senaj answered running his hand down his face.

"Do you know how surprised I was to see her face instead of yours? Do you know how surprised I was that she was in here telling me how she's been fucking my man instead of my man telling me how my kids are doing? Do you know how surprised I was to hear that you are going to be a father yet again?" Reign yelled.

For the first time Senaj looked at Christina and noticed that she had a small pregnant stomach. Senaj felt himself getting dizzy and couldn't believe how bad his luck had gotten.

"You didn't want to tell her, Senaj, and I thought that she needed to know." Christina said, trying to sound innocent.

"You sneaky, conniving bitch! How dare you? There is nothing to fucking tell." Senaj said seething through his teeth. Christina was lucky Senaj was not a woman beater because if he was, she was going to regret what she had done once he beat her bloody throughout the hospital.

"So, you are telling me the night of her grandmother being shot, you didn't get drunk off your ass and texted me to come get you from Smalls?" Christina asked, folding her arms across her chest with a smug look on her face.

Reign sat up and swung her feet over the bed, causing Christina to take a few steps back. She laughed a deep laugh and said, "I knew you were lying but I gave you the benefit of the doubt because you never gave me a reason to think of you as a liar. I cannot believe this shit."

"Reign, if you would just listen to me. Yes, I lied. I got drunk with Rasheed and Polite. With all the shit that had been going on, I needed it. I sent a text message that I thought I was sending to you. The whole time, from when I sent the text up until Akuchi had told me about Nana, I thought that she was you. I would never ever do no shit like this to intentionally hurt you or put you in this predicament."

"See, Senaj, that's the thing, you didn't hurt me. You ignited a fire in me that I have never felt before and I can't wait until these doctors discharge me. Both of ya'll are dismissed."

"Reign—" Senaj began.

"No, Senaj. I will text you when they give me a day to let me out."

Christina smirked because at that moment she felt like she was the victor of the two. She walked toward the door a little too happy.

Senaj grabbed her by the arm and said, "Wipe that smile off your face. You will never have me. It will always be Reign. You don't know what you've done and if you have that baby, I'm signing all of my rights away."

The color drained from Christina's face as she looked between Senaj and Reign. Senaj, without another word, walked out of the hospital room and Christina saw a sly smirk on Reign's face. Christina flew out of the hospital like a bat out of hell. Reign sat on the bed once they were out of the room and began to cry and laugh at the same time. Reign told a bold face lie when she said that Senaj didn't hurt her. Her heart broke into pieces, but this was different than the heartbreak she felt with Josiah. This was so much different. She didn't like it at all. She laid on the bed, clutching her heart as she allowed the tears to fall freely from her face onto her pillow.

***

"Senaj, you okay, bro?" Akuchi asked when Senaj had gotten into the house from visiting Reign.

He loosened his tie and took it off, throwing it onto the couch. He went to go find Zariyah and Kahlil, and when he found them, they were sleeping soundly in their cribs. He went back inside of the living room and took a seat on the couch.

"I've never wanted to lay my hands on someone so bad until this current moment." Senaj said clenching his hands open and shut.

"What do you mean? We saw the trail on TV and saw that you won. What's going on?"

"Where are the twins?" Senaj asked.

"They went to get some dinner."

"Reign is up."

"Word? When does she get to come home?"

"I don't know, and I think when she is able to, she won't be coming back here."

"Why?"

Senaj exhaled and pinched the bridge of his nose. He hated to have to repeat what happened, but he was at the point of not knowing what to do and he needed the help. He said, "Christina was in the room telling Reign every fucking thing. Oh, and she's pregnant."

The juice that Akuchi was drinking flew from his mouth and went half way across the room. He said, "With your baby? Please, Senaj. Don't tell me you were that stupid."

"I was drunk. I wasn't in my right frame of mind. It wasn't about me being stupid. I honestly thought that she was Reign. I told Christina if she was to keep the baby that I would be signing my rights away."

Akuchi stood up from the place he sat and went inside of the kitchen. He grabbed a beer from the fridge and sat back down. Slowly he opened the beer and stared a hole in Senaj.

"So, because you were drunk and thought that she was Reign, that's an excuse for you to ditch a child that belongs to you. Because of a female? You get to be a dead-beat dad because you fucked up one time and you're afraid to lose her? Senaj, help me understand your reasoning because you have absolutely no problem with taking care of Kahlil and he's neither yours or hers. How do you get to leave this baby without a father?" Akuchi asked. Granted, he didn't have kids, but despite men who leave their kids without giving them a chance, he didn't want his brother to be one of those men because Senaj wasn't built that way.

Senaj was speechless. No matter how selfish he wanted to be, he knew that his brother was right. He loved Reign with everything in him but if he had to admit it, he said what he said to Christina out of anger. His head began to hurt at all the hell that was unfolding.

Senaj said, "Since you have all of the answers, what do I do now?"

Taking a swig from his beer, Akuchi stood up and said, "That's for you to figure out. I can't always help you figure things out."

When Akuchi walked out of the living room, Jackie and Jamori came back with pizza. Zariyah began to cry so Senaj went to go get her. He needed to be alone with his thoughts. He needed to figure things out before Reign came home.

Chapter Three

Finding out that her boyfriend, her man, the love her life had cheated on her was the most devastating thing that could happen to her. Sure, almost losing her life and her child's was challenging, but God was on her side and they both lived through it. But this? This was something that she didn't know if she could come back from.

Hours after Senaj had left, Reign signed herself out of the hospital. It went against doctor's orders of course, but legally they couldn't hold her. And if they tried, Reign already had a number that she wouldn't have a problem dialing to shut that shit down if need be. With everything in her, she wanted more than anything just to go home and see her kids, but she had something to do before she made it known that she was home.

Everyone minus Jackie, who just so happen to pull up at the right moment. Reign climbed into the Escalade that Jackie had rented, and they pulled off.

Jackie snuck a look at Reign and smiled. "I am so glad to have you back. I couldn't deal with being around those niggas anymore." Jackie said while laughing.

Reign sighed and said, "How are the kids? Especially Zari-yah because I know that she's had some complications."

"She's keeping everyone on their toes, and she has all of the men wrapped around her little fingers."

"I can't wait to see her." Reign said with a smile.

"Now that's out of the way, please tell me what the hell is going on? Why are we riding out to Westchester county and why couldn't I tell anyone that you signed out of the hospital? Everyone has been worried about you. Especially Senaj. That man took a leave from work and everything just so that he could be there with the kids."

Reign grew tired about hearing Senaj. Everybody thought that he was just some faithful good guy. Reign thought so to until she found out he cheated. Before the tears threatened to surface, she said to Jackie, "Senaj had everybody fooled. He's not as perfect as everyone thought he was."

"Reign I—"

"Please, Jackie. I don't want to talk about Senaj. I need to focus on this task at hand."

Jackie looked at Reign again and decided to drop the issue. That was for now anyhow. Just because Reign didn't speak about it, Jackie knew exactly why Reign was upset. It seemed like Senaj wasn't listening to Akuchi's words and it was bothering him. So, of course he turned to Jackie about the situation and it was her who told Akuchi to let him know that Senaj would have to figure it out on his own. She told Akuchi that he couldn't continue to hold his hand. It was time for Senaj to fix his own mistakes.

Forty minutes later, they made it to their destination. They pulled up to a one-story brick house that sat on top of hill on Euclid Avenue in Ardsley, New York. They slowly crept past the house and noticed that all the lights were out but there was a car in the driveway.

Jackie continued a little further up the hill and made a U-turn. She parked the truck under a thick brush of leaves and branches that hung low from the trees.

Reign climbed into the backseat and opened the duffel bag that Jackie brought with them. Reign changed out of the scrubs that the hospital had let her leave in, into black jeans, a black hoodie, and all-black Converse. She placed the hood on her head and grabbed her rose gold twins, placing them in her lower back. There was a fresh tube of her favorite Christian Louboutin lipstick at the bottom of the bag. A smile spread across her face and she couldn't be happier to see it.

When Reign was done and geared up, she looked at Jackie and nodded. They headed down the hill and to the house that they just passed by.

"Real quick, Reign. I know you may be hurt by what Senaj did, but he is a good man. What he did was a mistake and you should really reconsider whatever you are thinking." Jackie said.

Reign sighed and said, "Jackie, have you ever been in love before?"

"No."

"Okay, so please don't try to give me advice on anything you don't know nothing about. I don't mean to sound harsh, but it is what it is."

Jackie didn't want to say anything else about the matter anyway. She gave her two cents and that's where it would end.

In silence, they continued to walk to the house. They ascended the stairs and onto the porch. Reign walked up to the window and cupped her hands over her face to peer inside. It was complete darkness. Reign looked around the porch for a flower pot, rug, or something that could give away that there could be a key hidden in or underneath it. There was none.

Reign and Jackie walked around the side of the house and into the back. Walking onto the deck as quiet as they could be, they saw multiple flower pots and a rug. Reign signaled for Jackie to start looking for a spare key. Jackie found one seconds later under the rug and handed it to Reign.

"I know you don't have an attitude about this Senaj thing?" Reign whispered, looking at Jackie's furrowed brows.

"Hell no. That's your situation. I gave my opinion. I just want to know why the hell you haven't told me why we are here and who's house this is." Jackie whispered.

"Remember the cop that shot Senaj?"

Jackie nodded.

"This is his house. Him shooting Senaj is why we are here." Reign placed the key in the lock and the door opened effortlessly.

They entered the kitchen and moved throughout the house looking for Burke. To be a male and living alone, his house was surprisingly clean. That was until they came across one of the bedroom doors. As they opened the door, a smell almost knocked them back out onto the porch. They used their hands to try and mask the smell. It was a mixture of liquor, throw up, and old food.

On the bed was Burke with pizza boxes, filth, and only God knows what else. There was barely any space to walk on the floor, but they managed to get through to the bed. Reign took one of her guns form the small of her back, and with the butt of the gun, she slammed it down hard on his dick and balls. Pain ripped through Burke's body as he sat up howling.

"Shut your ass up." Reign said, aiming her gun at him.

"What the fuck? Who are you?" Burked asked. He was a bit drunk. He had been drinking since he was found guilty. His sentencing day was coming the following week due to the judge giving him time to get his affairs in order. He didn't have anything to get in order, so he figured that he would spend his last free days drunk.

"Get your ass up and head to the living room." Reign barked. She wanted to be as far away from that room as possible.

Burke began to protest until he finally saw the gun that was damn near down his throat. He did as he was told and took a seat on the couch. Reign asked Jackie to walk to the truck to grab the duffel bag.

"You can't get away with killing a cop." Burke said with a chuckle. He thought by him throwing that in there, Reign would freeze up and let him go. He had stared death right in the eyes quite a few times but what he didn't know was that he was dancing with the devil. That is if the devil was a female.

"That's the thing. I've killed before and have been getting away with it. Just because you're a cop don't mean shit. There are cops like you who shoot unarmed black men and get away with it all of the time."

"Is this about that case with me shooting that nigger at the hospital? If it is, you're just a little too late. I go in next week to start my time. I don't show, they will question his family until they get answers. It will come to the light that you are behind this, and guess where you're going? Straight to where I am. So, you might as well cut me loose and let me serve my time."

"That is not enough for me. That man you shot is the love of my life. You could have taken him away from so many things. His family, his career, and it was all because of what? Because you're racist?"

"My life was in danger!" He yelled. That's what his lawyer advised him to say if he was to be approached about him being a racist.

Jackie had come and she was accompanied by a chair form the kitchen.

"That's bullshit—"

"It's not!"

"I was there when you shot him! If you felt like your life was in danger, then why didn't your partner feel the same way? I've waited for this moment since that day and I only hoped that you confessed that you were a racist."

With strength that Burke didn't expect, Reign grabbed him by his collar and forced him to sit on the chair Jackie brought into the living room. Reign passed her gun to Jackie so that she could go through the bag that Jackie had packed. She found some duct tape and began to bound his legs to the legs of the chair. Grabbing his arms, she taped them at the wrists behind him.

"Make it quick and to the point." Burke stated accepting his fate.

"Oh no. That's not how it's going to go. You don't get to have any power or control in this situation. I hold all of it." Reign said. She held her hand out towards Jackie and she reached into the bag.

Jackie pulled out a ten-inch meat cleaver. She passed it to Reign and watched, seeing that the instrument in her hands brought a smile on her cousin's face.

"What is it that you want from me?" Burke asked. His heart was pounding through his chest. Once he saw the cleaver come out of the bag, he knew that she was going to make him suffer before he died.

"I only want for you to pay for every black man you shot. The ones that died as well as the ones who lived, including my man." Reign circled around the chair before, without much warning, she slammed the cleaver down and instantly his toes were separated from his foot.

The blood curdling scream that escaped his mouth could be heard miles away. Jackie walked into the kitchen to get the small dish rag that she had noticed on the side of the sink.

"This little piggy went to market. This little piggy stayed home. This little piggy had roast beef. This little piggy had none." Reign said reciting the nursery rhyme while holding his toes up. They were barely being held together by bone and muscle.

"You sick bitch!" Burke was able to yell before Reign stuffed the rag into his mouth, taping it shut.

Once she made sure that it was in there, she went after his other foot. Ripping his shirt with the cleaver, she went inside of the bag again and found a small torch. With another smile placed on her face, she ignited the torch and placed the flame against his chest. She watched as his skin melted and burned. Reign held the torch against his chest and stomach until he suffered from third degree burn. By this time, he had lost consciousness and stopped squirming.

"Okay, let's pack up and get ready to leave." Reign stated.

"What if he gets up?" Jackie asked.

"He won't. I fucked up with James not making sure he was dead." Reign took her gun and placed it against Burke's forehead, sending one through his thoughts. For good measure, she aimed it at his heart next and sent one through his heart, leaving a clear entrance and exit wound. Satisfied with her work she untapped his hands and grabbed his hands. Taking out her lipstick, she drew a heart on his wrist. She felt herself becoming alive again.

While Reign went around the house, she wiped down everything that they could have possibly touched while Jackie packed the bag. As fast as they came, they left once the deed was done. Dropping a body always put Reign in a euphoric state and she suggested that her and Jackie went to go get a drink in celebration of her being back to her old self. What she didn't know was that there was a storm brewing at the home front.

***

Senaj paced in the living room while Akuchi and Jamori watched. Reign's doctor called Senaj to let him know that Reign had signed herself out of the hospital, but when she didn't show up at home, he started to worry. He called her nonstop, but she didn't answer. They eventually put two and two together when Jackie hadn't made it back from the store like she said she would. Akuchi began to call Jackie while Senaj called Reign.

"Ya'll know the reason why they not answering so ya'll might as well stop blowing up their phones." Jamori stated.

"I know why which is why I am. For all I know she could be giving Christina a C-section and throwing my unborn child down a sewer." Senaj said dramatically.

"Bro, stop worrying. They've been trained to know how to handle themselves. They good." Jamori stated with a chuckle.

Senaj side-eyed Jamori and continued to pace and call Reign.

Ten minutes later, now close to one in the morning, Reign and Jackie walked in giggling like two school girls. They appeared to be drunk and oblivious to the three men sitting in the living room.

"Shh. We don't want to wake them up." Reign said placing her finger against her lips and full out laughing.

Akuchi and Jamori smirked while Senaj stood there scolding them like he was their father.

Jackie turned to the living room and saw them in there. She said, "Oh shit, too late."

Reign took one look inside of the living room, saw Senaj and instantly sucked her teeth.

"Reign." He said.

"Nigga, please." Reign stated as she threw up her hand as if she was dismissing him. She headed to their bedroom and he followed right behind her, closing the door behind him.

"We need to talk."

"Yes, we do. But right now isn't good. I am past my limit of intoxication and this conversation won't be good." Reign said as she winced while taking her pants off.

"You shouldn't have left the hospital."

"And you shouldn't have cheated. But look where that has us."

"That's not fair, Reign. It wasn't intentional. I didn't just go out one day and decide to cheat. It happened exactly the way I told you it happened."

"How and why was her number in your phone?" Reign asked. Obviously, to her, Senaj was planning on doing something because why else would he have her number saved?

"Because—"

"I don't even want to hear it. What's done is done and that's it. I want to move past this, Senaj."

"Before we do, I need to tell you something."

"You cheated again?" Reign asked, grabbing some clothes to take a shower.

"No. Hell no. That was one mistake that won't happen again. I'm pretty sure that one day you will forgive me but—"

Reign exhaled because she really didn't want to have any conversation with Senaj. She just wanted to shower, sneak a peek at her kids, and sleep her drunkenness off. She closed her eyes before she looked over her shoulder. She said, "Senaj, I just want to shower and kiss the kids goodnight. Please, can we have this conversation in the morning?" Reign began to walk away but if Senaj didn't get this off his chest now, he felt like he would burst inside.

He had a lot of time to battle himself over what he would do in the situation with Christina. His decision could possibly ruin any hope of them working out their relationship. Before Reign was fully out of the roomm he blurted out, "Reign, I'm going to take custody of Christina's baby upon a DNA test proving that I am the baby's father."

Reign's heart, no matter how drunk she was, dropped to her feet. She couldn't believe what he just said to herm let alone think that this was going to work afterward. Of course, if he kept his word by giving up his rights, she would have been by his side. Her mind sped through things to say but she was rendered speechless. She looked over her shoulder once again, causing Senaj to feel like a complete ass. The tears that cascaded down her face in warp speed spoke volumes to his heart. Hurting her was the last thing that he wanted to do, but somehow, he still managed to do so.

"You keep her child, me and mine are gone." Reign finally responded. She kept her eyes trained on him to make sure that he understood her.

From the look on her face he knew that she was serious, and it was his turn to have his heart drop to his feet.

**Lipstick Killah 3: The Finale
Coming Soon!**

Submission Guideline

Submit the first three chapters of your completed manuscript to ldpsubmissions@gmail.com, subject line: Your book's title. The manuscript must be in a .doc file and sent as an attachment. Document should be in Times New Roman, double spaced and in size 12 font. Also, provide your synopsis and full contact information. If sending multiple submissions, they must each be in a separate email.

Have a story but no way to send it electronically? You can still submit to LDP/Ca$h Presents. Send in the first three chapters, written or typed, of your completed manuscript to:

LDP: Submissions Dept
Po Box 870494
Mesquite, Tx 75187

DO NOT send original manuscript. Must be a duplicate.

Provide your synopsis and a cover letter containing your full contact information.

Thanks for considering LDP and Ca$h Presents.

Coming Soon from Lock Down Publications/Ca$h Presents

BOW DOWN TO MY GANGSTA

By **Ca$h**

TORN BETWEEN TWO

By **Coffee**

BLOOD STAINS OF A SHOTTA **III**

By **Jamaica**

WHEN THE STREETS CLAP BACK **III**

By **Jibril Williams**

STEADY MOBBIN

By **Marcellus Allen**

BLOOD OF A BOSS **V**

By **Askari**

LOYAL TO THE GAME **IV**

By **T.J. & Jelissa**

A DOPEBOY'S PRAYER **II**

By **Eddie "Wolf" Lee**

IF LOVING YOU IS WRONG... **III**

LOVE ME EVEN WHEN IT HURTS

By **Jelissa**

DAUGHTERS OF A SAVAGE **II**

By **Chris Green**

SKI MASK CARTEL **II**

By **T.J. Edwards**

TRAPHOUSE KING **II**

By **Hood Rich**

BLAST FOR ME **II**

RAISED AS A GOON **V**

By **Ghost**

ADDICTIED TO THE DRAMA **III**

By **Jamila Mathis**

LIPSTICK KILLAH **II**

By **Mimi**

WHAT BAD BITCHES DO **2**

By **Aryanna**

THE COST OF LOYALTY **II**

By **Kweli**

SHE FELL IN LOVE WITH A REAL ONE

By **Tamara Butler**

LOVE SHOULDN'T HURT

By **Meesha**

Available Now

RESTRAINING ORDER **I & II**

By **CA$H & Coffee**

LOVE KNOWS NO BOUNDARIES **I II & III**

By **Coffee**

RAISED AS A GOON I, II, III & IV

BRED BY THE SLUMS I, II, III

BLAST FOR ME

By **Ghost**

LAY IT DOWN **I & II**

LAST OF A DYING BREED

BLOOD STAINS OF A SHOTTA I & II

By **Jamaica**

LOYAL TO THE GAME

LOYAL TO THE GAME II

LOYAL TO THE GAME III

By **TJ & Jelissa**

BLOODY COMMAS I & II

SKI MASK CARTEL

By **T.J. Edwards**

IF LOVING HIM IS WRONG…I & II

By **Jelissa**

WHEN THE STREETS CLAP BACK I & II

By **Jibril Williams**

A DISTINGUISHED THUG STOLE MY HEART I II & III

By **Meesha**

PUSH IT TO THE LIMIT

By **Bre' Hayes**

BLOOD OF A BOSS **I, II, III & IV**

By **Askari**

THE STREETS BLEED MURDER **I, II & III**

THE HEART OF A GANGSTA I II& III

By **Jerry Jackson**

CUM FOR ME

CUM FOR ME 2

CUM FOR ME 3

An **LDP Erotica Collaboration**

BRIDE OF A HUSTLA **I & II**

THE FETTI GIRLS **I, II& III**

By **Destiny Skai**

WHEN A GOOD GIRL GOES BAD

By **Adrienne**

A GANGSTER'S REVENGE **I II III & IV**

THE BOSS MAN'S DAUGHTERS

THE BOSS MAN'S DAUGHTERS II

THE BOSSMAN'S DAUGHTERS III

THE BOSSMAN'S DAUGHTERS IV

A SAVAGE LOVE **I & II**

BAE BELONGS TO ME

A HUSTLER'S DECEIT I, II

By **Aryanna**

A KINGPIN'S AMBITON

A KINGPIN'S AMBITION **II**

I MURDER FOR THE DOUGH

By **Ambitious**

TRUE SAVAGE

TRUE SAVAGE II

TRUE SAVAGE **III**

DAUGHTERS OF A SAVAGE

By **Chris Green**

A DOPEBOY'S PRAYER

By **Eddie "Wolf" Lee**

THE KING CARTEL **I, II & III**

By **Frank Gresham**

THESE NIGGAS AIN'T LOYAL **I, II & III**

Mimi

By **Nikki Tee**

GANGSTA SHYT **I II &III**

By **CATO**

THE ULTIMATE BETRAYAL

By **Phoenix**

BOSS'N UP **I , II & III**

By **Royal Nicole**

I LOVE YOU TO DEATH

By Destiny J

I RIDE FOR MY HITTA

I STILL RIDE FOR MY HITTA

By **Misty Holt**

LOVE & CHASIN' PAPER

By **Qay Crockett**

TO DIE IN VAIN

By **ASAD**

BROOKLYN HUSTLAZ

By **Boogsy Morina**

BROOKLYN ON LOCK I & II

By **Sonovia**

GANGSTA CITY

By **Teddy Duke**

A DRUG KING AND HIS DIAMOND I & II

A DOPEMAN'S RICHES

By Nicole Goosby

TRAPHOUSE KING

By **Hood Rich**

BOOKS BY LDP'S CEO, CA$H

TRUST IN NO MAN

TRUST IN NO MAN 2

TRUST IN NO MAN 3

BONDED BY BLOOD

SHORTY GOT A THUG

THUGS CRY

THUGS CRY 2

THUGS CRY 3

TRUST NO BITCH

TRUST NO BITCH 2

TRUST NO BITCH 3

TIL MY CASKET DROPS

RESTRAINING ORDER

RESTRAINING ORDER 2

IN LOVE WITH A CONVICT

Coming Soon

BONDED BY BLOOD 2

BOW DOWN TO MY GANGSTA

Mimi